Healing Crystals & Other Breakables

Gwen Tolios

Libra Chai

Contents

1. Healing Trauma — 1

2. Daddy's Little Girl — 6

3. Training Ground — 9

4. Rival Mourning — 11

5. Dollmaker — 15

6. Undine's Paladin — 17

7. Rewind — 32

8. Fairy Wasp — 34

9. For the Love Of Animation — 37

10. Nightshift Woes — 44

11. The Corner Monster — 48

12. Celestial Healing — 55

13. The 12-Month Cold — 57

14. Wet In Emergency — 71

15. The Letter Thief — 73

16. Aphrodite's Feathers   76

17. Intrusive Thoughts   86

18. Wrong Guess   89

19. Birthday Bakes   93

20. The Goddess Of Modern Marriage   99

21. Agatha's Curse   102

22. Three Raindrops   108

23. Unconditional Love   109

24. Rowdy Children   119

25. Etched in Brass   121

26. Addictive Meditation   131

27. Selkie Business   135

28. Till Death   138

29. To Hold You Again   143

30. Baking Rites   146

31. Mothman, Bigfoot, & I   151

32. Rider's Three   156

33. Previous Publications   164

35. About Gwen   166

Healing Trauma

I became a healer for a reason. It's traumatic, no need to get into it, but like most who enter the profession I did so because once upon a time I wanted to heal someone and couldn't. Like I said, it doesn't matter who and it's a common enough tale.

What does matter is what I learned that day. Energy is finite, and you need a lot to heal. A. Lot. And even if you give it your all, it may not be enough.

We specialize, healers. Potion makers, diagnostic spells, illnesses, or quest medicine. I know someone who specializes in skeletons; she can take one look at you and read every broken bone you've had. I know another who has created wellness charms so strong they keep you from getting sick for a year. A third who knows poisons inside and out, to detect the undetectable and negate it.

I focused on energy storage. I put crystals in my ears, wore quartz bandoliers, topaz beads on my wrists. I filled them all with energy, bit by bit. Feeding myself into them, then resting so I could fill another. Saving for when a major healing was needed.

I'll admit it became an obsession. I needed larger energy reserves, and thus more crystals. When the party I joined suddenly had two barbarians the obsession became worse. What if one cleaved the other in a rage? What if a bar fight happened hours after a monster fight and my crystals hadn't been replenished with the energy I needed?

It worried me, and I gave more of myself to the crystals than I should have.

"Stop," my party, my friends, my family said. "You're pushing yourself. You're draining your energy too fast."

That scared me. I'd seen what happens when a healer drains it all. No one survives, the injured or the healer. That couldn't be me. I needed to be there for them. But to be there for them I needed crystals bursting with magic.

I let them convince me to take a vacation. We visited a monastery and the monks were kind. Good food, good people, and plenty of time to breathe and meditate. Feel nature all around us.

Touch it.

Snag it.

Birds, it turned out, could fill crystals too. And grass. And dogs and mice and freshly bloomed wildflowers. We left the monks with my energy replenished and my crystals thrumming.

Two weeks later, we came across a dragon. Its acid breath made it hard to breathe before we were in strike range. We coughed, our rogue tried to hide the blood on her lips, and I knew this battle would be tough. Chronic damage, chronic healing, and who knew what we'd need when the battle was done.

"I'm taking point," I said, healing my family's lungs as I touched them on my way to the front, striding into the dragon's acid. I covered my face and mouth, touched my newly emptied crystals, and reached for the largest source of energy.

I don't think the dragon knew what I was doing, not at first. It blinked in surprise at how quickly it ran out of acid, roared in confusion when it struggled to dodge barbarian axes.

As the party tells it, my crystals glowed, then started to crack. This is when the dragon targeted me, when it tried to slash my belly open and crack my skull.

I don't remember its attempts. My party getting in the way, the roars. Only pulling on the dragon's life force and shoving it into my crystals as they emptied to heal my friends from the impact of aerosolized acid and claw swipes. And yet, dragons are so powerful, so magical, I slowly built up a surplus.

Crystals crack when they're overloaded. Mine shattered one by one, shards digging into my skin even as I healed each cut with the released energy.

The rogue went to her knees, thinking I hosted a god, but no. It was just me, stealing the life of a dragon. I needed the energy, needed it stored, you never know when the next injury will be.

But eventually, my crystals were gone and the only storage container was me.

I lost my mind. Did things I didn't think I could, attacking the dragon with my bare fingers to get at its life force. Breaking my nails pulling at its scales, only for them to grow back as I healed the damage moments later. I didn't recognize my family, their pleas for me to stop, or their cries of worry when my heart stuttered and stopped and restarted until the dragon died and there was no more energy for me to steal and cycle into my body to heal the damage.

I dropped.

They sobbed.

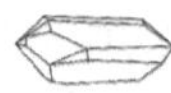

I can't *not* collect energy. Not now that I know it's everywhere, that I can steal it from anything, that I can store and use it within my body, damning the consequences.

Like I said, all healers have trauma and you can't leave that behind in your village. I will always, always need an energy stockpile.

But we have rules now. There is a cap on my crystal collection and my rogue keeps count. There is a potion in my alchemist's bag, designed to block the sense I use to detect outside energy and pull it me. My barbarians take turns leading and covering, and there's an effort at plans other than charging in to minimize injuries. I'm never allowed to stride forward to lead the group, eager to strip away the life of an enemy for the sake of my family.

I'm supposed to be a healer.

I'd do it again for them, of course. But since they don't want me to, I resist. I stay back, watch them fight, and keep my crystals full.

Daddy's Little Girl

You limit the time your daughter spends looking in the mirror.

"It's not healthy," you tell her, "Watching mortals all day."

"Not all mortals," your daughter replies. "Just one."

"That's even less healthy. You shouldn't be so obsessed with a mortal. They die."

"This one's different! She doesn't age."

You snatch the mirror from her, and she pouts.

"Go play, Time," you command. "Or study."

With a sigh, she storms out of her room.

Once you're sure your daughter has gone, you use the bronze-framed mirror yourself.

It's the same girl as always, if twenty is a girl. Long curly hair, blue tips this time, eyes hidden behind black cat eye glasses. They don't do a very good job hiding her old, tired eyes.

You brought her back at least twenty times.

You didn't regret it the first time. Time had cried and cried, unable to find her favorite human in the mirror. You thought nothing of using your powers to bring the girl into view, and only after she showed up pale and covered in blood did you realize what you'd done.

You brought her back to life so your daughter could watch her, like fixing a broken toy.

Your wife scolded you. Life is a gift given only once, she chastised, but you didn't need the reminder. Death is also only given once, a final gift of peace after Life's bubbles of torment. You were upset and guilty you took it away from the girl and promised no more meddling.

But the next time the girl disappeared, Time cried for hours. So you brought her back, a repaired teddy bear. A renewed show, but with a shrinking episode count every season. The time between the girl's death got shorter after each demise.

She shouldn't be alive, and in your role as Death you felt the darkness of your realm pull at the girl constantly. Yet Time kept searching and you would do anything for your daughter.

You made the girl immortal.

No aging. No illness. No wounds. Her invulnerability has made her more interesting to Time, who spends more and more hours watching her. Who from afar sees not a source of entertainment, but a person she's grown to cherish. Love. Imagine being with as a fellow Force.

But as the girl gets more interesting to Time, she turns more destructive toward herself.

On the surface of the mirror, you watch her tie up her curly hair and step into a plane. Watch her subtly damage the parachute. Watch her fall, hit the ground, bounce, glasses cracked and lenses shattered on the grass around her. Watch her cry and sob and know this is her third attempt this year. It's June.

The suicide attempts are accelerating. It's a miracle Time hasn't seen one yet; you snagged the mirror just in time.

You might not next time.

You don't want your daughter to watch someone she's come to love try to destroy herself over and over again. You don't want your daughter to learn it's your fault.

But you also can't bear to take the girl away, to see Time cry when she can't gaze at her love.

This perversion of her realm has already driven your wife away; Life can't look at you. But Time does and you can't give that up.

Not now. Not yet.

In the mirror, the girl staggers to her feet and walks away. Ever youthful. Ever healthy.

And like you, ever tormented.

Training Ground

It's an odd little corner, the intersection of 1st Avenue and 2nd Street. The intersection of 5th Avenue and 2nd Street is full of churches. And 1st Avenue and 6th Street is a collection of car dealerships.

But 1st and 2nd is the public service corner. The public library with its frosted windows. The municipal center with a tiny parking lot. The elementary school, with its blacktop painted in yellow lines for foursquare and baseball. And the McDonald's, a public service because it's McFlurry machine is miraculously always working.

I don't know why those machines break so often. Or why this location not only never has a broken machine, but it also never out of an item, even those supposed to be temporary. A McRib in Janurary? Thank you very much.

It's enough of a miracle for me to ignore the extreme squint of the woman who takes my credit card or the way her lisp is evident on 'thank you' and not 'small soda'. Ignore the flicker on the back of the hand of the person who hands me my order making his hand look purple to match his contacts. How the toys in kids' meals are never quite right, molded in strange poses or constructed from the wrong material. We once got a superhero toy carved out of smooth, oiled wood.

Everyone needs to start somewhere, and wrong toys and odd staff are worth year-round soft-serve mixed with mini M&M's.

Rival Mourning

I t's a sadder turnout than you expected. Sure, a funeral for Captain Gray would bring a lot of people, but Graham Jones had been unnoticed. Too focused on saving others, rushing away to answer screams, to hold a steady job or build a circle of friends.

You blame yourself for some of it - it was your algorithms that detected crimes and buzzed his watch. Once or twice you silenced it so he could sleep, but the extra hours of rest simply made him more eager the next day. He was Captain Gray, you were Black Hat. He was the hero, you were the man in the chair. You'd always been his enabler, just like he'd always been your muse for new tech and code.

Graham's funeral is attended by you, Graham's older neighbor, the one friendly connection he'd made at his current job, and the barista from Graham's local coffee shop. She'd introduced herself as Stacy and said ever since she'd caught Graham putting salt in his coffee four years ago she'd teased him about it mercilessly.

The funeral is quick and generic at the funeral home chapel. There's no burial, but you're handed a cream box with ashes afterward.

Stacy is the only one who stays long enough to watch you receive it.

"You should spread his ashes on the ComBank building."

You had planned on that, snagging a building key-card and sneaking into the rooftop garden. Graham had liked to end patrols there. In the absence of stars, he'd look at the lights in the various buildings. They didn't twinkle in the same way, but they brought him a sense of peace you could feel over the comm line as you chatted in the late night hours.

Stacy should have no reason to suggest spreading Graham's ashes there. You narrow your eyes and pull Graham close.

She's wearing a T-shirt with the coffee shop logo, but as she pulls her long hair back into a bun she exposes her earrings. They're 4mm gages, hand painted with a stylized falcon.

It's the symbol Kestrel has stamped on her suit.

You tense. Captain Gray had stopped one of Kestrel's plans three months ago. If she's here for revenge, you're sunk. You can't fight. You wish the pastor, or anyone who works at the funeral home, would walk into the room right this second. It goes unfulfilled.

"Why are you here?"

Stacy shrugs. "We weren't friends. I never wanted to be, even when I figured out who Graham was. But

I'll miss him all the same. And... I know how it is to lose a partner."

"Merlin."

They'd been twin birds of terror two years ago.

"My sister. Died of complications after a fight with Hooper."

You wince. Hooper is a hero, but the most aggressive in town, fighting with serrated metal rings. The papers only call him a hero because he stops crimes, versus his morals or altruistic heart.

"It's tough," Stacy continues, "losing a partner. You do everything together. No one knows you better. Keeps all your secrets. It can get... lonely... without them."

You brush the plastic urn. She sounds so sincere you believe Stacy is her actual name. You remember sitting at your station last night, watching crime occur because there was no Captain Gray to aim at the criminals. And when you cried at the third mugging the cameras flagged, there was no one to grieve with - you hadn't built a social circle either.

Any masked work can build the most beautifully intimate relationships, but it can also be the most isolating thing in the world. You carry all of your secrets and Graham's by yourself now.

Well, no. Stacy knows some of Graham's secrets too.

Stacy holds out a business card, logo for the coffee shop bright yellow on a pale blue background. "I work here. If you ever wanna talk. Feel less alone. We might have been enemies, but Gray would check in on me. Ask how I was doing between blows. And while he never figured out I knew, he'd do the same thing as Graham, worrying over the bruises or brace I'd display in the coffee shop. You don't fight, Black, but I'm guessing we are both addicted to caffeine."

You take the card, more sure about that than the offer of friendship. She smiles at you. You try to smile back.

"Don't get sucked in," Stacy says. "Screen breaks are healthy."

"I'll keep that in mind."

Kestrel and Captain Gray had been enemies for six years, but Stacy's face is honest in its worry and care. Her lips twitch into a sad smile before she leaves.

Kestrel has been flying solo since Merlin's death, and you wonder what this means for you. Can you direct another hero? Can you watch the city's crime from afar and not want to do *something* to help?

You step outside the small mourning room just in time to watch her push open the door to the cool March air, ponytail swinging, and figure a latte would be a great breakfast tomorrow.

Dollmaker

"The best way to keep safe is to make something not want to kill you. It prevents murder and accidents."

My nana would say that to me every time she tucked me in. Her nana had told her the same thing. It was why my mother had my crib in the doll workshop, among the fake hair and dress scraps. When I got too big for that, she had me sleep holding tools of the trade.

"Show them you will be useful," Mom would whisper as she rocked me, taught me how to clean plastic bodies, and follow a pattern. "Useful things are kept in good repair."

I stitched rice-filled girls and painted the lips of porcelain creatures. Washed plastic hair and brushed it till soft. I watched spirits practice the art of possession, bursting seams instead of skin and exploding glass instead of eyes. And they, in or out of a possessed object, watched me repair their mistakes.

If they needed to learn fine motor control, I built a doll with fingers. If they wanted something familiar,

I asked their opinion on the color to use for hair. If they needed to learn how to fit in something small, I created stretchy limbs.

My nana and mother never said it out loud, but I knew it was only a matter of preference that the spirits practiced with our dolls and not our skeletons. They could destroy me whenever they wanted, sliding into my body wrong or taking a misstep that sent me falling down a flight of stairs.

They let me live so I could serve the needs of future ghosts. And I chose not to exorcise them to keep my family alive.

I grew up with spirits, learning beside them, and they developed alongside me in turn.

It kept both families safe.

Undine's Paladin

Seledyth slowly stripped herself of her armor, placing the pieces in the waiting arms of the councilman. Periodically, she looked out into the harbor. The water was smooth, the rowboat tied to the dock barely rocking, with no evidence of bad weather on the horizon.

"Can you describe again what you and the villagers see?" she asked, unbuckling her chest piece.

The councilman bit his lip, gaze darting nervously to the water. "Restless spirits, the priestess says. She rows out to the middle of the harbor every year to say rites for those with underwater graves to prevent them from lingering. But this year, after the ceremony, they started appearing. Wispy human torsos floating over the water that glow. You'll see when night hits."

Seledyth gently hung her chest piece on the man's extended arm. It might be as thick as hers, but her arm was corded with muscle and the councilman's looked to be padded with fish fat.

"Has the priestess performed rites again?" Seledyth knew she had, the temple had been her first stop, but the councilman calmed as he talked as if his nerves were attached to the words pouring out of his mouth.

"Every month for the past four."

She nodded. The priestess sent for aid shortly after the first failed attempt. *They are spirits whose graves lie underwater but are resistant to the rites. Something caused their deaths that the rites do not address, and until the cause can be identified and prayed for, they will continue to be visibly restless.*

"Have there been more storms than normal?" Seledyth looked out toward the ocean, peeling off her visby gauntlets.

Mox'tan was a small village but had a large, natural harbor and a reputation for asking no question of ships who sought shelter for a few nights. It made the town a popular port, but entry was difficult. The opening was well guarded by rocky pillars, only some of which jutted out of the water, and ancient ruins that withstood saltwater and sea life. Storms would make navigation riskier than normal.

"No," the councilman said. "But the storms are killing more people, and smaller rainstorms that usually don't pose a problem have caused losses too."

"Hmm." Perhaps something had recently inhabited the underwater ruins at the harbor's entrance and hunted during the storms. "Thank you. Take care of my armor while I'm on the water." She stepped down into the rowboat. It rocked but settled as she sat on the bench to grip the oars.

The councilman looked at the metal hanging off him and piled in his arms, which were starting to tremble. The armor of a paladin was considered an artifact of their chosen god; an honor to touch, and a curse to mistreat.

"Of course, Paladin." He bowed as much as he could with his burden. "Anything special about its care?"

"Keep it dry. Saltwater is corrosive and dew can lead to rust." She pushed away from the dock. "If I don't return, give it to the priestess."

Seledyth belonged to Chamenos, the god of the lost. Forever lost, part-time lost, lost in your mind, lost in the world, Chamenos was there to soothe you and help you find your way.

Restless spirits, those lost in traveling between this world and the next, fell into Chamenos's domain. Local priestesses and their rituals were usually enough to calm them, the songs outlining the path to the beyond with Chamenos's light. Seledyth never heard of a priestess not able to sing a soul to peace.

She rowed toward the harbor mouth, her back to the sun and wind. She ignored the bits of brown hair escaping her braid and the occasional flash of golden light on a nail head, too busy concentrating on navigating around the anchored ships and the harbor entrance. As she passed by a mid-sized merchant's boat, she heard the muffled singing of the crew. She smiled at the memory it evoked - the celebration on a ship she'd sailed on a year ago after guiding it to port after two days of storms had blown them off course.

Guiding lost ships were bittersweet missions. After all, no paladin had been on board to help her parents' fishing boat come home.

As Seledyth headed toward deeper water, the sun-warmth she'd felt on the dock faded with the setting star.

Slowly, the restless spirits the councilman mentioned appeared. They were as described, wispy torsos hovering over the water giving off a soft glow. Below each would be a body, the only thing they hadn't lost in the world, and hopefully evidence of what had happened.

Seledyth stopped rowing and drifted on the water, the far-off cry of sea birds filling the air. She tried to make out the features of the spirits around her, but the fading sunlight and water reflections blinded her. No matter, she had a list of the dead from the priestess. She'd simply wished to see if there was a pattern to the deaths other than *died at sea*.

The boat bobbed as she scanned the harbor. Most of the spirits were in the harbor, but a few were near the entrance over the submerged pillars and ruins. Each spirit was silent, which made the slap of water on the side of the rowboat echo. She shivered.

This felt wrong, but nothing registered with mortal senses explained *what* or *why*.

Time to ask for help.

Seledyth moved from the row seat to the center of the boat's bottom, sitting cross-legged on the damp wood with a hand on either knee. There, stitched in the fabric of her leggings, was the symbol of Chamenos. The Right Way. The Life Lighthouse. The Guiding Light. The Path To Return. Names and depictions varied, but at its core, the symbol consisted of a slender trapezoid with a circle on top.

"This paladin is lost in her task," Seledyth said, "and seeks Chamenos's aid."

On the edge of her senses, she felt Chamenos turning their attention on her, even as her sense of self retreated. She wasn't Seledyth, she was a vessel, something Chamenos could occupy and use to help those who needed it.

"I'm lost in knowing what these souls need to move on."

Seledyth closed her eyes, took a deep breath, and was no more.

Occupying a mortal body, Chamenos opened her eyes and was drawn immediately to the lost souls anchored to their graves. They shimmered the glow of the newly dead, and from the tapered end of each torso ran a line to a body on the ocean floor. Chamenos leaned over the side of the boat to follow glowing thread. Each body at the other end was weighted, be it with stones or wreckage. While some of the older bodies had been picked apart by fish, the newer ones were simply bloated.

"What do you need?" she asked the soul closest to her. "Why can you not find your way to peace?"

Reaching over the side of the boat, she plunged her hand into the spirit.

A fierce possessiveness filled her. The spirit was protecting something, clinging tightly because nothing else mattered. *Mine, mine, mine*, the man repeated.

Ah, tied to a material gain, Chamenos thought. She rowed to another, reached inside the soul to hear the answer to the same question. *Mine, mine, mine.*

You can't have it!

It's mine!

Each soul clung tightly to something she couldn't identify.

"You don't need it anymore," she tried to say. "You won't need it beyond."

None of them believed her. *I need it more than anything.*

She tried to change tactics. "It's yours. You can bring it with you."

I won't let go.

"Can you show me it?"

No! You can't have it!

"You are lost. Why are you here? Why can you not move on?"

I can't, not without –

The boat rocked, and with it Chamenos's body shifted, her left hand moving from knee to boat for balance and -

Seledyth blinked, once again in control of her body, mortal mind processing what it could, mortal body aching from hosting a god. There was no time to recover because the boat rocked again as something hit it. Carefully, she looked over the edge.

The water was dark, inky and deep. She couldn't peer through it to the ruins below, to the bodies Chamenos had seen, but there was a shift in the water. A shadow circled the rowboat.

Seledyth sat still, following the shape's course when it came into her vision. It was long, with a tapered end. Seconds passed, the shape got larger, and Seledyth noticed the spirits around her had moved. Anchored to their bodies, they couldn't travel far, but they'd shifted as far as their tether allowed.

What circled her was the thief the spirits worried about.

She assumed the spirits hadn't followed the instructions in the priestess's rites because they focused on the wrong death, drowning instead of say, killed by a creature. If that had been the case, Seledyth could have either informed the priestess of the correct instructional rites to perform or done it herself. But Chamenos had seen no mutilated bodies under the water, and the answers they received indicated the spirits were lost between worlds due to a strong desire to protect something. What it was, Seledyth didn't know, but before she could guide them to the next world, she had to get rid of the threat they felt in this one.

Unfortunately, it hadn't just been her armor she'd left on shore, it'd been her sword, too. All she carried was a candle, flint, and a dagger. Considering this creature was capable of sinking small boats, a dagger wouldn't be enough to kill it.

Seledyth frowned, rubbing the palm of her hand over her knee as she thought. She needed a net and maybe an extra pair of hands to help throw it and haul the creature into the boat. Nothing for it. She'd have to go back to shore. Seledyth stood, ready to walk the two steps to the bench to sit and row when the creature slammed into the boat.

It rocked wildly. Seledyth widened her stance, wobbled, and evened out her balance just as the boat was hit again. She toppled and a third, more vicious hit flipped the rowboat over and sent her underwater.

Cold seeped into her limbs, not enough to be a risk, but startling enough she gasped and swallowed water. She kicked toward the surface, the ghosts above bright stars leading the way, and broke through coughing. A few feet away floated the overturned rowboat. Seledyth swam toward it.

The hull was too rounded to heave herself onto, but she clung to the wood. Night had properly settled in, the dregs of sunset gone, but in the light from the spirits she saw the two oars being pulled quickly away.

Seledyth stopped kicking and let her legs droop, concentrating on holding onto the boat. It'd be best to conserve her energy.

She pressed her skin against the boat's bottom, disregarding the slimy wood and doing her best to ignore the salty taste in her mouth, and waited. She wasn't lost and couldn't call upon Chamenos, but even if she was, turning her body into a vessel was dangerous. She'd have to keep at least one hand on her knee, minimizing her ability to hold on to the boat and kick her legs. Plus, she already ached from hosting the god not even thirty minutes ago. No, Chamenos was a last resort.

Something brushed her calf. A brief touch, but firm. The creature wanted Seledyth to know it was there.

She resumed kicking, hoping to avoid a leg grab while surveying what little she could see. A shape rose from the water at the bow of the boat.

The top of a head, then a face, then shoulders. Upon the dark water, lit only by the glow of spirits, Seledyth couldn't make out enough details to identify the creature. The water on its skin glistened, and it looked feminine with full lips and a heart-shaped face. Neither were distinguishing features to identify a water creature by.

It opened its eyes, which glowed an eerie green and spoke. "Would you trade for a rescue?"

Water dripped from its mouth, the *glug* of it falling making the first words hard to understand, but Seledyth could guess. She stared at the creature, certain it had made this offer before. Certain it had been denied by the spirits tethered to bodies in the harbor's seabed.

Still, she had to ask.

"What do you want for a rescue?"

The creature lifted a hand, one that seemed human except for how it formed from the water instead of connecting to the creature's shoulder.

"Your soul."

No wonder the spirits had been so possessive. No soul, no afterlife. They would have clung, were clinging, very hard to their souls.

"I'd rather keep it," Seledyth said.

"You'll get tired," the creature said. "You'll slip below the water. Swallow it. Drown. I can flip the boat. Put you in it."

"Return the oars you stole?"

The creature grinned. There was a distinct lack of pointy teeth, which was the last clue Seledyth needed to name it.

An undine.

Water spirits who took on the form of humans, almost obsessive in their mimicry of humanity. With bodies made out of water, shaped at will, they were near impossible to kill without drying them out. In a deep harbor connected to the sea, Seledyth had no chance. She could make it flee, but not destroy it, and that wouldn't allow her to complete her mission – lead the restless spirits to the path they needed to the world beyond.

"Why do you want a soul?"

The undine floated in the water, staring at Seledyth with glowing green eyes. She got the sense the undine was surprised to be asked. No doubt, the others had all given emphatic nos.

"Do you want...to eat it?" Seledyth guessed. She wanted answers soon. She could feel the cold seeping into her skin, cramping her fingers and making it hard to hold onto the hull.

The undine disappeared. Seledyth tracked it by how the spirits hovering over the water moved, each one eager to avoid the reason for their halted journey. The undine made a wide circle before resurfacing under the spirit closest to Seledyth.

With the slightly better light, Seledyth could see the undine's face. It looked like the spirit above her. Then, as Seledyth watched, it morphed to features eerily like her own.

"I want to go where the woman sings about."

"The woman?"

"Who came in on a boat like yours, but at dawn, with lights around her feet."

The priestess. What had the councilman said, the lost spirits had started showing up after the yearly ritual for the drowned?

"You want to die?" Seledyth asked, confused.

The undine scrunched up her face.

Right. To elemental beings, as immortal as their element, death probably wasn't a concept.

Something in the undine's face was familiar though, and not simply due to the creature wearing Seledyth's features.

"You're lost. You don't know how to get to where you want to go."

The undine blinked. "No. I know how to get there. The woman sings it. But I need a soul. I will save your life if you give me yours."

"If I give you mine, then I can't go either."

"I will take it!" the undine gurgled, spitting water.

"A hundred souls light these waters, and they flinch from you. If you could take one of them, you would have."

The undine sunk beneath the water, and Seledyth felt rush of cold on the back of her knees. Then, tugs on her feet as the undine removed her boots.

A minute later, the undine crawled on top of the boat's hull from the other side. Her weight shifted it, but not enough to risk Seledyth's grip. Standing tall, looking down at her while wearing Seledyth's boots, the undine was vaguely see-through and glowed the same green as her eyes. She looked like Seledyth's water reflection, a perfect replica down to the wet strands of hair.

Seledyth knew undines had an obsession with mimicking humans, but what if it went beyond that? What if it wasn't mimicry, but desire? To be human? To have an immortal soul?

The undine had replicated Seledyth's clothing, including the embroidery depicting Chamenos's symbol. Would those work?

"Chamenos," she said, reaching toward the undine's knee, "I need your aid guiding this lost creature. She desires the world beyond, but cannot find her way."

When Seledyth's hand made contact with the water image of her sewing, her hand went through the undine's body. It still provided enough contact for Seledyth to feel her god's attention, the rush of their power and concentration filling her body.

Chamenos looked inside the creature she touched and found it empty, screaming. It had been striving for something for so long but had only recently realized what for and every attempt to get it had been thwarted. *I want it! I need it! Make myself whole!*

"Oh, you've been lost all your life," Chamenos said. "Aching for something you do not have, adrift in the world. Are you all like this?"

It was the cosmic sense of being lost. Knowing that the universe was so vast, and you so small. That others would linger, and you wouldn't.

Guide me! The undine's void screamed. *Fill me! Help me!*

"Souls cannot be made," Chamenos said, "but they can be shared. Paladins offer theirs to me, and I offer this one to you."

"Share?" the undine asked.

"Take her hand," Chamenos said as she faded away.

Seledyth blinked away her god, the sudden drain of energy making her sag against the boat's hull. Her arm dropped through the undine's calf, exiting the water version of Chamenos's symbol. Before it could hit the wood, the undine caught her hand.

It didn't feel like holding a hand at all, more like sticking her hand in a pool of water.

"I have your hand! Share!"

Seledyth blinked up at the undine. Her body ached, so tired she could barely be bothered by her cold, wet clothing. But she remembered what Chamenos had felt from the undine, and while its loss wasn't the same, Seledyth could remember asking for guidance at a lighthouse years ago. There'd been no temple of any kind in her small fishing village, so she'd had no one to cry to, no help in understanding her parent's death.

Chamenos had answered back then. Just like Chamenos continued to answer Seledyth's requests for aid over the years. But she struggled to understand what Chamenos meant by soul sharing, how to help the undine.

I give my life and soul to Chamenos, the god of the lost. We are two in one body. I am but temporary, a vessel for the eternal guiding force. Words from her oath swirled in her head and with them the oaths of a different ceremony. A rite she had both administered and seen performed during her travels, spoken over a couple holding hands. *We give our lives and souls to each other. Two people, one heart, one hearth. Bound by the gods and us.*

"There's a rite. The priestess has to sing another song, binding us."

"The song will give me a soul?"

"It will grant you access to mine."

The undine didn't cry, she couldn't being made of water, but Seledyth knew what her own crying face looked like.

"We don't know what it will do to you. Taking my hand."

"I don't care. You'll share your soul?"

"I'll share my life."

Around them, with a sigh, the spirits of the lost uncoupled from their bodies and rose toward the stars.

Rewind

I t's deja vu. Groundhog Day. A time loop. But at the same time, you're not sure if that's the right comparison because everyone knows the day is repeating. Everyone is trying to do something different, which makes it not that dissimilar from before the Rewind. People are still unpredictable.

What isn't is the earthquake.

Every day, at 12:22 pm the tremors start.

You can hide someplace new each time, hoping to avoid an injury. You can spend the morning rearranging your belongings, preventing a floor covered in shattered china. You can evacuate to watch the building fall, you can try a new route to escape the city.

You remember each time you're stuck in the head and crash to the floor. Every walk over broken porcelain. How the building collapses on you from different floors and different sidewalks. How the bridge splits and sends people to the water.

You remember every mistake and its consequences, but so does everyone else. Maybe a spot that kills you won't another. Half the city knows the bridge will be lost.

You all know the Rewind is real. You all know you can change the day. You're not going mad.

But you can't change nature. The earthquake will always happen. The shift in plates is predictable and unstoppable. People die and are reborn after periods of darkness. You have stared at the abyss more times than you can count.

Sometimes, you wish the dead would stay dead. Let people rest. Let them enjoy their escape or kill their useless hope. Let the Rewind not happen at 2:22 pm, resetting 12 hours.

Let the next loop be successful not if you live, but if you see 2:23 pm. The Rewind is not a thing of nature like the magma under the earth. You need to find the person who hits the button and kill them. Find the machine and smash it.

The earthquake is predictable.

You are not.

Fairy Wasp

You know a little about garden fairies. No one wants to be the victim of small curses, but it's nearly impossible to know what sets a fairy off so they're often treated like wasps - you ignore them and they'll ignore you.

Still, half-dead chrysanthemums can't be a nice home.

You buy a new pot full of blooming flowers, putting it right next to the old one. The fairy investigates it from time to time, you can see them harvesting nectar, but they continue to live in the half-dead pot.

Thinking it might just like the placement of the pot, you rotate the two. The fairy stays with the now-dead chrysanthemums. It thankfully doesn't seem to have too much against the move; you don't think you've earned a curse, anyway.

In the evenings, you sit on your balcony and enjoy the sun. Sometimes you see the fairy, sitting outside the burrow it created in sun-baked potting soil. You don't know where it goes during the day; they're supposed to feed on nectar but your one pot of healthy chrysanthemums can't be enough to feed it. Does it harvest from your neighbor's mini roses? The posies three floors down? You've never seen it fly from or to your balcony, but it is nothing more than a tiny, green speck the size of a thumb joint.

It sticks around as summer ends, and you start to get worried. You know it's not a pet, dependent on you for care, but the flowers are dying with the season and with it the fairy's food source. You leave out caps of honey water, and now, after nearly two months of you and the fairy mutually ignoring each other, you have attention.

It's nerve-wracking, watching the fairy land on your hand while you're reading a book. Can you turn the page? Or will that upset it, leading to a stinging curse? You don't turn a page for a solid ten minutes until it flies off to its burrow.

When you step outside it sometimes flies around your head, wings buzzing in your ear.

One evening, you place the cap of honey water not near the pot, but on your small bistro table. The fairy lands next to it, slurping the water. You've never seen it drink before, and try to hide your laughter. Faires are delicate, magical creatures and you expected them to use their hands as a cup. But no, the fairy ducks its head into the cap, slurping. When it sits back on its knees, water drips from its chin. Its hair, really wisps of magic, is weighed down.

It looks at you with round, faceted eyes and sings. You tense, fairies only make a sound when casting magic. Have you finally pissed it off? Have you been cursed?

Slowly, you step back into your apartment. Your bowl of raspberries, which you'd been munching on, is once again full.

You've not been cursed, you've been blessed.

You cry, glad the fairy likes you that much. Trusts you that much.

It's just a magical wasp, you try to tell yourself. It feeds on flowers. They die when the weather gets cold. You shouldn't feel so connected to what many people consider a pest.

You grab a shallow dish, fill it with more honey water. A feast for a fairy. Slowly, you carry it and your bowl of raspberries outside.

The fairy is on the table's end, legs dangling and wings flapping like a butterfly. Its gaze zooms in on the dish. You can't read its facial expression, but you think clapping hands are joy. You set both dishes on the table, and for the first time, enjoy a meal together.

For the Love Of Animation

I probably shouldn't be bending to my student's wishes, but I only got my degree and teaching license three years ago so we're peers. I took the bet that I could teach a statue to pass as human at the year-end banquet.

Animating a statue isn't hard - just a tiny push of magic. They're zombie-like in their steps, knees not bending right and arms often locked in the position they were carved into. I ask my students to donate an outfit to the practice statue in the classroom, and before long she's dressed in someone's stretch dress, a dark blue beanie, and some giggling soul slips on a pony bead bracelet.

The stone woman looks ridiculous, which is what makes her the best statue on campus. The students name her Dove, for the soft grey of her skin.

Dove doesn't do much. She patrols the classroom, and even as she gains more clothes from my students to hide her stone skin, it's obvious what she is by her gait.

I muse on how to teach her human fluidity as I watch her patrol between lectures. She doesn't see like humans. She can't watch me bend my knee. But she must have some perception - Dove responds to commands and can handle stairs, if badly.

I watch her stumble-lurch into my lecture hall from the hallway. She turns toward the stadium seats, ready to climb them as she performs her sentry duty. On a whim, I call out to her.

"Wait."

Dove stops before the bottom stair, waiting as I step close. She's acquired enough pony bead bracelets they clatter as she walks, but her legs are still bare. She doesn't have the flexibility to put on a pair of pants, but someone has placed slipper socks on her feet.

"Walk slowly," I command, and as she moves I run my finger up her thigh to her hip, sinking magic into the stone as I recall old anatomy lessons. Thigh muscles relax as the hip pivots to lift the foot high for the stair, re-engaging with each footfall.

I climb the stairs with her, using magic to trace the use of tendons and muscles in each leg. At the top of the stairs, I crack my back and step out of the way, letting Dove continue her path.

I watch as she walks the narrow band of floor before the top tier of seats, then descends the stairs on the other side.

Not human. But closer.

I want to praise her, which is silly. The work is mine; I directed the magic into a smooth gait, it's my power that allows her to ambulate. I want to smile at Dove and say 'good job'. I can't bring myself to do it, but my students are quick to praise her as they come in.

To them, Dove is a puppy I'm teaching tricks, not a construct brought to life via magic. Experimental magic at that.

Statues are supposed to fill in the ranks of an army. They're a temporary defense of the city to give the citizens time to evacuate or get to shelter. They're supposed to be active for days at most. Running with the idea that the longer a statue is active, the smoother its movements, I've been feeding her magic on and off for six weeks.

There's a paper in there somewhere, a study I can publish and use toward tenure. It's too soon however if I want to win the bet of convincing strangers at the banquet Dove is human. No need to announce what I've done, what I'm doing, until summer break.

Dove's walking doesn't get better, but it doesn't get worse either. I continue to give her bursts of magic regularly, and once we get to that part of lessons my students give her trace amounts as practice. Sometimes it's too much, I can feel the buzz of magic in Dove's body threatening to crack stone.

I help her deal with it by distributing the energy into the ends of her - fingertips and the frozen curls of hair. The carved eyelids and the boots on her feet. I push magic through her hands, following imaginary tendons. I circle her lips, trying to mimic the feel of my smile.

Dove's footsteps are smoother, and she turns her head now. Her arms swing like a power walker's, but they match her stride. I start to think I might win the bet.

Halfway through the year, I see Dove fidget. She's standing near the door, watching, but there's a slight lean she does every so often I realize is her shifting her weight from foot to foot. It's a behavior she's learned on her own, and the thought shocks me enough I stop mid-lecture.

"Professor?" a student asks.

I shake my head. "I just thought of the perfect comeback," I say and they laugh before I continue talking about defensive magic.

When Dove cuts across the lecture hall on her path, none of the students blink an eye. It's such a common occurrence. But for the first time, I notice her walking gait is smooth. Completely human.

Her arms are still stiff, so I use the time between classes to direct the current of magic in the stone through her arms. Guiding her through arm swings and elbow bends and a shoulder roll. She turns her head to watch my fingers run over her stone skin. I know it's my imagination filling in the sensation of breath on my cheek, but it's there all the same.

She's flexible enough in her movements she could put on a new outfit, one hiding stone skin. Paint, or a veil, could hide her stoney cheeks. At this rate, if I bring Dove as my date to the end-of-year dinner, no one across a room would clock her as an animated statue.

She could probably learn how to dance.

One morning, I open my front door to find her on the doorstep. She could have followed me home, but I hadn't heard her behind me yesterday. Our eyes lock. Hers don't have pupils, but I know she sees me in her own way.

She raises a hand to wave.

I stammer out, "Good morning, Dove."

She doesn't say anything back. Her throat is carved from limestone. She doesn't have a tongue to move. But even her light grey skin can't convince me she's a living statue sometimes. She walks so smoothly over flat ground and stairs. She moves around a child. She keeps pace with me on the way to campus. She turns to look at me, tilts her head.

She doesn't smile, but I can feel it. I smile back.

Dove shadows me around campus, drawing attention. Usually, she stays in the building where I teach and hold office hours. Now she follows me as I head to lunch and attend staff meetings. The pony beads on her hand don't clack because she moderates the momentum of her arms. Her beanie hides her stone hair. Her, by now filthy dress, doesn't draw much attention. Not as much as the sometimes loud *thump* of her steps.

Some people double-take - staring at her exposed grey legs. Others don't.

Dove is just another body in the hall to some of the students. She waves to some of the frequent attendees of my office hours, and I can't quite convince myself it's because she knows who has donated magic to her existence over the months.

I don't hear anything from my colleagues or my boss, but I imagine the conversations to be had tomorrow. I worry over them on the walk home, Dove keeping pace. Would they want me to explain what I did? Do it again? Would they, would they take Dove?

I look at her. We're waiting for the light to cross and the golden rays of the evening sun reflect off Dove's face. Whoever carved her did a wonderful job.

I brush a hand across her cold cheek, depositing a bit of magic. I close my eyes slowly, focus on the feeling, and try to share it. Try to imagine Dove's grey face coming to life, eyelashes fluttering, hair twisting in the breeze, lips parting.

She will never speak. Never breathe. Never age, though her stone may whether. But she's alive enough to me.

The light turns, and I cross the street. Dove walks beside me, and I feel the cool touch of stone. I look down and watch her twine our fingers together. I stare as she lifts our linked hands to her cold lips, as they twitch in an attempt to kiss the back of my hand.

It's rough, of course it is, but it's so light I can imagine it's real skin. Chapped to high heaven, but real and alive.

Dove tilts her head like she had that morning, and I know she's smiling. I know she's talking, even if I can't hear it. She tugs me forward, and I follow.

I've lost the bet with my students, the game has been discovered. But I feel the magic beneath Dove's skin, artificial veins that give her life, and it feels like winning.

Nightshift Woes

"Jack," Kevin calls from across the restaurant.

Jack tenses, it's never good to hear your boss address you with that tone.

The restaurant owner cuts in between Jack and the pair of guys who'd just walked in. "I apologize," he says with a smile. "I'll take you to a table. Jack, my office."

Jack bites his lower lip to keep his emotions from his face as he heads to the back of the restaurant, ignoring the curious looks of diners. He has no idea what set Kevin off, but he's never seen the man tense like this. Even when Veronica broke half a dozen mugs, he'd been sympathetic and checked her hands before reaching for a broom.

A minute after Jack settled into the extra chair, Kevin storms into his office. He doesn't wait to take his seat before cutting into Jack. "You're fired. Between this being your second time late this month, and what I just saw, I cannot keep you on staff."

Jack wants to protest – he can't predict when or for how long a railroad crossing will be closed and he has no idea what has set Kevin off – but his boss's stern face and clenched fists tell him this is not a fight he'll win.

"Fine. Have these back." Jack digs into his apron and pulls out his gun and badge. He slams them both on the table, relishing in Kevin's jump. Losing this job will suck, but hopefully, he can find something before his next rent check is due.

Kevin stares at the gun. "What the fuck? Have you had that every shift?"

Jack halts his plan to storm out, slamming the door closed hard enough to rock a photo off the wall. Instead, he blinks at Kevin. "Yeah? Sergio gave them to me my first night shift."

"And you just accepted?" Kevin shrieks. His face, red just moments ago, is now pale.

Jack throws up his hands. "You pay really well for a twenty-four-hour coney island, so I already figured you were a front for something illegal. The gun's not loaded and the badge I think is from a stripper costume."

Kevin's face furrows and Jack's voice tapers off as his confusion grows. "Sergio said it was just to scare off people," he finishes in a mumble.

Kevin rips his gaze from the gun to look at Jack. He closes his eyes and takes a deep breath, letting it out slowly before speaking.

"Jack," Kevin leans forward and locks eyes with him. "I pay well because I value my employees. I promise you, this isn't a high-risk job. It really is just seating customers and cleaning tables. Wait, is that why you asked the two guys who just came in to show their package? I thought you were asking them to strip!"

Jack shakes his hand and hands, denying the idea with his whole body. "What, no! It's not uncommon for guys to come in at night with bulky things under their shirts. When they do, I ask them to prove it's not a gun. One of those dudes had something under his arm hidden by his jacket."

"Stay here."

Jack pouts, but waits as Kevin heads back into the restaurant. He throws his head back, staring at the drop ceiling. It looks yellow, a detail hard to see during his usual night shift. Jack holds back a yawn. With two people out sick, Jack had volunteered to help out during the day. Night owls tip well, but there's less of them.

He rolls his neck, eyes landing on the gun and fake badge. He's beginning to realize that for all that the lunch hour is more hectic than any late night rush, night shift is probably the crazier one.

Kevin comes back into the office. "The guy did have something under his clothes – a book because he didn't want it to get wet in the rain. I also talked to Carl."

"The line cook?"

Carl doesn't work overnights, but he comes in early for the breakfast shift. Jack's hours overlap with his by an hour or two, depending on the number of hungry people who show up.

"He also has a fake gun and badge from Sergio."

Kevin sounds exhausted, but Jack is not going to turn down the chance to keep this job.

"If I'm not fired, you can wire me with a button camera and I'll record all my night shifts for the next week so you can try to catch what Sergio is doing as the night manager."

"You don't know?"

"All I know is that it's dangerous enough he thinks I need a gun, but I'd like to know the particulars of that, yeah."

"Deal."

"And if I find stacks of money somewhere, I want a bundle. Hazard pay."

Kevin sighs. "If it doesn't end up as evidence for the cops, sure."

Jack stands before sliding the gun and badge back into his apron pocket. "Good enough. Now if you'll excuse me, I'm sure there's a table that needs bussing."

The Corner Monster

I t was raining. Not hard, but enough to be annoying. Enough Cath should have stuffed her hands
in her pockets and power walked home. But no, *coffee!!!* the impulse gremlin in her brain screamed. So
she bought some from the coffee shop near school
and stubbornly drank from it as she ambled down
the sidewalk.

Each time she tilted her head back for a sip, raindrops splashed on her face.

She wished she'd never gotten it. Trapped in her
aluminum thermos, it couldn't warm her hands and
it also failed to warm her belly as she walked. But it
was in her hand, she paid for it, she was gonna drink
it and *oh.*

She stared at a house down the street. Really.
Was the neighborhood going to start decorating
for Valentine's Day now? Her family had just tak-
en down the Christmas tree, she refused to hang
strings of red lights and put up – *dear god.* Was that
an inflatable cupid?

Cath stepped closer, sipping her coffee. The thing
looked half set up, puddles forming in the nylon

while the ground under it quickly turned to mud. Good luck to whatever dad had to fix that once the rain stopped.

She tipped her head back for a larger sip, crossing the intersection. Two blocks to go, she thought, eyes closed as she felt the rain beating on her cheeks.

Honk!

Cath jerked. She'd stopped just before the curb to savor the caffeine and rain. She wasn't in danger of being run over by the car approaching the intersection, but quickly scurried up the curb. The car sped by, splashing her with enough water to soak her jeans. Cath jumped backward, coffee sloshing over her hand.

Sighing, Cath watched coffee and rain drip down her fingers. The small triangle of grass she stood on, rapidly turning into a mud puddle, bubbled as it absorbed the coffee drips.

Feed the mud monster! Her thoughts shouted.

Giggling, she tipped her thermos to pour out a thin stream.

Mud traveled up the coffee and yanked the thermos out of Cath's hand. She stared, not quite sure she wasn't hallucinating, as she watched the mud swallow the container whole.

The taste of coffee lingered in the back of her mouth. It still dripped from her fingers.

Cath did what she should have done twenty minutes ago – shoved her hands in her pockets and walked home with her head down and hood over her head.

She felt off doing dishes that night. She used the same thermos every day. Filled it with coffee in the morning to take to school. Filled it with water at lunch. Maybe coffee for the walk home, if she got a craving. But here it was, chore hour, and she had no thermos to add to the washing in the sink.

She scrubbed at a plate, waiting for someone to ask where her thermos was, but no one in her family noticed it gone.

Cath lay in bed, worry keeping her awake. What would she use tomorrow?

She usually chose a different route to school each day, alterations based on whether something caught her attention or if she'd turned at the second street too often that month. But the next morning, Cath walked the same way she had through the rain the afternoon before.

There, on the grassy corner, lay her thermos.

She could pick it up. Take it to school and wash it out in the bathroom sink. But as she imagined doing so, she remembered mud running up the line of coffee, filling the thermos, and yanking it down.

Grab it! It's yours! Your favorite.

The cap had come free, leaving the thermos open. The mouth was partially submerged in a shallow pool of muddy water, hiding the metal lining underneath.

She reached for it. The mud inside the thermos bubbled and popped near the metal rim. Cath snapped up to her full height.

The mud monster could have it.

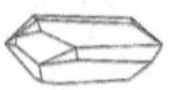

Cath felt off the whole day, just as out of sorts as washing dishes last night. There was no coffee to sip during homeroom. No cool water during math. There was always one less thing in her hands than expected, leaving her unbalanced. None of her mom's options had felt right in her hand that morning. She tried browsing during lunch for a new thermos, she'd get the same brand. Same color.

Except, the thermos had been a gift and as she stared at the online listings, she realized she didn't even know how to start filtering the thousands of options.

"Cath!"

She jumped, finding her friends exchanging glances over their lunches.

"Everything alright?"

"My thermos got stolen yesterday."

"Do you know by who?"

"Yeah."

"Are you gonna ask for it back?"

Cath hesitated. What if the mud monster didn't just take her thermos? What if it took her? She imagined mud traveling up her hands, her arms. Slimy and cool, until the smell of loam filled her nose as it covered her face.

Cath shuddered. "No."

She went back to browsing the options for a substitute on her phone. None of them looked right.

It'll pass, she told herself. *You'll find a new favorite. Eventually. Just...order five of them, see which you like, and return the rest.*

She filled her cart, but her mind kept drifting all afternoon. Her thermos in the mud. Her thermos in her hand. Muddy coffee. Muddy hands.

The images haunted her, imaginative hallucinations with a touch of memory. They lingered until she found herself staring down at her thermos after school.

No one had snagged it and the mud monster hadn't completely claimed it.

The impact of yesterday's rain was almost gone, thanks to a clear, sunny day. The cupid down the street was proudly inflated. From the corner of her eye, Cath could see more houses with red lights. The earth around her thermos had started to dry, the mud puddle retreating to leave the bright green grass exposed.

There was still soupy mud in the thermos, but there was no bubble, no monster, no evidence of something a thermos could sink into. If Cath stepped on the metal tube, she doubted it would sink more than an inch or two.

Or maybe the soft earth would claim Cath's ankle, pulling her down down down into the earth.

Coffee for the mud monster.

Cath for the mud monster.

She shook her head and continued to stare, waiting, she realized, for an impulsive thought to run through her brain and tell her what to do.

Nothing.

Her hand twitched. She'd missed the weight of the thermos so frequently in the past twenty-four hours. The smoothness of it against her palm. The crisp etched edge under her fingertips she idly traced at school.

She'd felt wrong-footed all day. Could she be wrong-footed tomorrow? The day after? All week? A month?

Cath bit her lip, the pain of it making her decision for her. She'd rather ride out the sharp bite of a tooth than feel so unbalanced.

"One," she whispered to herself, widening her stance.

"Two." She lifted onto her toes, ready to throw herself backwards or sideways or wherever to escape a mud monster's grasp.

"Three." Cath grabbed her thermos around the open mouth and yanked.

It came free easily. It hadn't been as deep in the earth as she thought. The mud hadn't fought to keep it. She could barely see disturbed dirt from where the thermos's lip had been buried.

Cath peered into the thermos. The mud inside was still sliding to the bottom, thick enough to stick to the metal sides. She rotated the thermos, mouth down, and waited for the mud to fall out in a single, sticky glob.

She'd cradled it to her chest and jogged home. She'd wash it twice.

Celestial Healing

There are things in the world that shouldn't be seen. The color of gravity. The shape of imagination. The physical bend of space-time. The texts sent between trees, the sighs between stars. These are not for us. They are the wrong sense, too grand and too small and too beyond our perceptions.

There are things in this world that shouldn't be seen, but we do anyway. The marrow of our bones. Agony on an infant's face. Black blood between teeth. Blue lines stretching up arms. Parasites in a petri dish. Half-eaten legs and wholly devoured eyes.

You can trade the experience of one for the brush of another if you can travel to the abandoned hospital halfway up the mountain. There, wait with your eyes closed until the air is so thick you can eat it. The Nurse will heal your break and provide you with the sensation of solar winds. Cure your poison and leave the taste of wonder on your tongue. Mend the ulcer and imprint on your mind the memory of ultraviolet. Hints of the celestial beyond that you will never, should never, experience.

Keep your eyes closed the entire night once you're at the abandoned hospital, keep your understanding of the Celestial Nurse to faint traces of touch. Not because the Nurse will remove her blessing, but because she is a thing that shouldn't be seen. And while seeing your insides might traumatize you, seeing hers will overwhelm and confuse your body so much it returns to stardust.

Which is a type of cure, I suppose, but not one that will return you to me. Remember that if you hobble up the mountain tonight and hear the heartbeat of a distant planet.

The 12-Month Cold

Cambre palmed open their door, waving to their friends in the hall, before confidently striding into their quarters. The lights blinked on at the motion, but as soon as the door slid shut Cambre barked out orders to the room's assistant.

"Lights, thirty percent."

They dimmed from their standard eighty and Cambre slumped. Feet flat on the floor, palms against the smooth metal of the door. Pushing weight down and behind, Cambre focused on those points of contact instead of giving in to the desire to melt. If they slid down to the floor, they wouldn't get up, and Cambre had things to do.

Brush their teeth. Shave. Change into pajamas. Crawl into bed.

Each task seemed ginormous, and Cambre had already done so much today. They'd worked a full six-hour shift. They'd walked the promenade several times.

Their legs were trembling, a pain throbbed behind their left eye, and Cambre hadn't smiled all evening for fear of blood on their teeth from biting their lips to prevent a wince.

"Your heart rate is fast," the room assistant said. "Let's walk through a breathing exercise together. I will count in for four, hold for two, and out for four. Start."

Cambre followed the instructions, half because the exercise usually worked and half because if they didn't, there was the risk of alerting Medical. Each room's assistant wasn't connected to the ship's main AI or surveillance system for privacy, but certain triggers would make the assistant connect to the broader network. Like sudden deviations from medical norms.

Cambre's room had learned whatever this slow-growing illness was with them, modifying their medical baseline with new data, but if their breathing didn't even out there'd soon medical staff knocking on the door.

Cambre couldn't risk that.

"Hold, two. Out, two, three, four."

Cambre breathed with the room's assistant, eyes closed. Their body still ached, but in privacy they let their muscles relax. It was okay if they trembled or let pain flit across their face. In their room, there was no one to hide from.

"Good! Your breathing is normal."

Cambre opened their eyes. "Gradually raise lights to fifty percent."

The room complied, making it easier to see the furniture and wrinkles in the rug. Cambre pushed off from the door but used the wall to steady themselves on the way to the bathroom. They took their time with the standard hygiene routine, even going so far as to take a shower. They had a feeling they wouldn't have the energy for it in the morning.

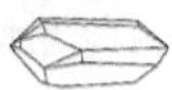

Cambre walked into comms the next morning and stumbled to the small replicator. Their morning struggles had become something of a joke, but morning grumpiness and neediness for caffeine were effective misdirects. Those were acceptable reasons to be a little late, be a little stiff, hold off on cheery 'good mornings!' and wince at the bright lights in public spaces.

No one on the *Sunspot* needed to know Cambre hadn't rolled out of bed just in time for work instead of an hour before, mentally preparing for the day and the gargantuan effort it had been to get to the bathroom. They were happy the crew quarters were tight; less steps to take.

Cambre collapsed in their seat, clutching steaming coffee. Usually they faked a yawn, but right now, all they could do was sit there and stare at the screen, not quite comprehending the display.

"Hey."

They looked up at Nicti. Her dark purple hair was pulled back tight enough to reveal the bony ridges forming half a ring around the back of her skull that all lilians had.

"You okay? We didn't stay out *that* late last night."

Now, Cambre forced the yawn. "I read late."

"Must be good if it kept you awake. What's the title?"

Cambre took a sip to buy themselves time. They'd been exhausted last night, but the pain had made it hard to drift off, too present to ignore. They'd ordered the AI to start a narration of something as a distraction. Cambre fell asleep to the drone of its voice, paying more attention to the rhythm than the words.

"I'll have to let you know later. The AI picked it for me. It was a romance."

Nicti didn't like romances.

Work dragged. Cambre felt heavy, the headache from last night making their eyes blurry. They ignored the display and put on a pair of headphones. Listening wasn't an uncommon method of classifying readings the ship picked up; some people swore by it, believing ears were more sensitive to noises than eyes in picking up and identifying the amplitude spikes.

There wasn't much to listen for – direct communications to the ship went to a different station. Cambre's job was to listen to the translated noises of space, years of training allowing them to detect quasars, black holes, and other celestial bodies as well as undiscovered patterns that may or may not be communications. The classified noises, with as much detail as Cambre could pick up, were sent along to various other teams. Navigation, Research, External Comms.

Eyes closed, Cambre tried to concentrate. Six hours, with a thirty-minute break in the middle. Just listen, classify, send. Listen. Classify. Send.

Their body was so distracting today. Sleep had done nothing for the cramps in their legs, and they hurt just sitting there. Cambre wanted to be back in their quarters and flat, cold cloth on their face to help with the headache and lights off. All they wanted was to rest, but they had to work.

A tap on their shoulder gave them a jolt – someone there to take over as Cambre took a break. They'd classified nothing in the past hour. They looked to their right – Nicti was gone, also temporarily relieved. Usually, Cambre joined her, but today they didn't feel like getting out of the chair, let alone chatting with a friend over lunch.

But if they didn't get up, if they gave a hint that something was wrong, there'd be a conversation with Medical.

"Haven't identified the most recent sound," Cambre said, passing over the headphones. "But it's far off so shouldn't be a worry."

"I'll figure it out."

Cambre gave up their seat, moving slowly and keeping their face flat. Today was *bad* but pain had also become a familiar feeling in the past year. Slow steps kept their gait even all the way to the break room, and then to the replicator to ask for lunch.

Something small that their stomach could handle – soup and bread.

Nicti looked up, halfway through her lunch, as Cambre placed their food down with more force than necessary. They couldn't help it, the weight of the tray heavy on their wrists. The break room was brighter than Cambre wanted it to be. Someone's laugh pierced their skull.

Stiffly, Cambre sat and started eating. Nicti never went back to her meal, something that looked like bright green risotto with an unfamiliar veggie in it. Instead, her eyes tracked Cambre's hands and it was so, so hard to keep the tremble out.

She reached under the table and put a hand on their knee. "What's going on?"

Cambre looked at her. "Nothing."

"I've seen you eat soup for lunch nearly every day for the past three months. You're wincing, which you did last night too."

"Nothing, Nicti."

"Liar."

Cambre looked back at their food. Felt the spasmodic twitch of their thigh. Nicti did too.

"If you're sick, Medical-"

"I'm not sick." Their voice was firm, almost loud in the breakroom. Cambre softened it. "I don't need to go to Medical."

There was a level of fitness required to live in space. Resources were precious, crews kept small. You had to contribute to the small, space-faring society with labor or funds. Cambre would deal with pain. The *Sunspot* was home in a way nothing had been before, and nothing would ever be.

Nicti removed her hand. "Are you sure?"

"If I was sick, my room assistant would have alerted medical staff."

And it would have if this was a new, sudden pain. If it hadn't gotten worse over time, baselines shifting in small enough degrees the change threshold never triggered. This wasn't some illness to recover from with a spot of medicine, this was a change in their body that threatened their career, their friendships, their life.

Cambre would suffer for it. Gladly.

Nicti looked at them, and Cambre pleaded with her in their head to let it go. To ignore the muscle twitch. Ignore the small meals and harder mornings. To respect Cambre's choice to do what they wanted.

But the ridge of bone around her head wasn't just for aggressive greetings amongst her species. They protected a ring of nerves dedicated to analyzing touch. Human fingers could detect nano bumps on flat surfaces, lilians could detect nano differences deeper. It made them good doctors. Or annoying friends. No doubt, Nicti had felt something more concerning than a muscle spasm. And unlike Cambre's room AI, she wasn't looking at month-over-month changes. She was comparing the Cambre of today to the Cambre of six months ago. A year ago.

"After our shift, we're going. Even if I have to drag you."

Nicti watched them the rest of their shift and when it was over, followed one step behind as they left the communications room.

"Are you walking to Medical, or am I dragging you?"

Cambre tried to glare but felt so tired. *Sleep, sleep, sleep* pounded in their head in time with their steps. Nicti offered an arm to lean on, but Cambre refused. Silently, they walked beside each other to Medical. Cambre clenched their firsts, not sure if the tremors were from anger or exhaustion. They couldn't remember anything they classified today.

At least Medical was closer than their quarters.

As soon as they walked in, a medical bed folded down from a wall. Cambre ambled toward it while Nicti waved to the lilian physician. He waved back, holding up a finger in a sign of 'please wait', and Cambre sat on the bed. Cambre tried to keep the relief from their face, but based on Nicti's worried look failed.

They forced themselves to act fine instead of giving in to what they wanted to do: nervous taps of their legs, squinting at the light, rubbing at a sore thigh or their forehead. They needed to be *healthy*.

They needed a doctor to tell Nicti her concerns were for nothing.

They needed to stay on the *Sunspot.* They needed to stay *home.*

The doctor walked over, smiling at Cambre before flipping open a tablet.

"Can I have permission to access your quarter's AI storage of your medical readings?"

Cambre wanted to say no, but a healthy person wouldn't do that. Mouth too dry to answer, they nodded.

The doctor worked on their tablet, typing and pressing and flicking screens down and sideways. He kept a passive look on his face, but Cambre watched the scrolling slow as the doctor digested the information. Cambre wondered what data was there – how often they came home exhausted? How often they dimmed the lights? The spikes in their pulse while doing basic tasks? They didn't think the AI could track pain, but were there recordings of Cambre stumbling to bed? Walking with the support of the couch? A count of the sheer number of times the AI had walked Cambre through a breathing exercise?

"Right." The doctor put down the tablet near Cambre's thigh. "It's obvious you're currently struggling. What do you need now to help you get through the day?"

Cambre curled in. They didn't want *anything.* They wanted whatever was happening to go away or be ignored.

"Nothing."

"Cambre," Nicti said softly.

Cambre ignored her, looking at the doctor. "I'm...I'm just sick. Like a cold. I'll be fine. I'll be better next month."

The doctor crossed his arms. "Most colds can be treated with quarter remedies: a steamer, tea, or cough syrup. Sometimes, I need to provide someone a stronger, prescription cough suppressant like codeine. Just until they're better, of course."

Cambre nodded.

"So," the doctor continued. "Would something temporary like codeine make your life better?"

"I-"

Nicti placed a hand on their thigh. She would not let this go.

If their position had been reversed, Cambre realized, they'd insist Nicti talk to Medical too.

"Yes," Cambre whispered to their knees. "A stronger painkiller." Had the AI recorded that too? How much naproxen they took a week? Or had that been in Cambre's medical file, noting how frequently they'd asked for a refill from the quartermaster?

"And what about something like a steamer? Do you need a device for occasional use in your quarters?"

"No."

"I'll write you a prescription for painkillers, just a step above what we give the crew to manage themselves. If you need something stronger, let us know." The doctor waited for Cambre's nod before continuing. "I'd also like to draw some blood. Make sure this cold of yours is really that."

"Do you have to?"

"Just let him look you over, Cambre!" Nicti threw up her arms. "I'm worried about you, okay? Let him do his job and *help*."

The doctor coughed. "Maybe if you wait outside, Nicti?"

She looked back and forth between the two of them. When Cambre refused to lift their gaze from their knees, she let out a long sigh and walked away.

After a minute, the doctor spoke. "She's right, you know. I'm here to help, but I can only do what you want me to. Refusing medical treatment is allowed, but if you deteriorate to the point where you can't perform your duties on the ship, you'll be sent planetside."

Cambre clenched their fist, thinking about all the sounds they hadn't classified this past shift. Was there no way to stay here? To share lunch with Nicti every day? Join their friends in the evening? Follow up with Research to understand a strange new sound they heard? To sit on the observation deck and stare at the stars for hours, content and at peace?

"I'm fine. I can work."

"Do you think you can in a month?"

"Yes."

The doctor sighed, gently placing his hand on Cambre's thigh. "Again, I can't force you to accept treatment, and I'm not going to hold you down to draw blood, but there are no bad consequence to letting me help you. If this isn't a cold, we don't know how your body will be months down the road. Maybe we could stop it, but only if we catch things early. There's been some amazing progress in gene therapy in the last five years."

Cambre stayed silent.

"Here are your options. You take the painkillers, which I'm guessing will only partially help, and gamble with your health down the road. Maybe this is as bad as it gets. Maybe it's not. But you look miserable to me and your weight is declining. My gut says it gets worse, and in a year your employment is terminated. Maybe you accept more help than just a prescription, say tinted glasses to help with your increased light sensitivity, and extend your time on the ship. Third option is you let me run a few tests. Unless what you have is super, super rare, I can identify it we can come up with a treatment plan. Make the leg tremors go away."

"And if you can't stop or reverse this, this cold?"

"Always a risk," the doctor admitted softly. "But knowing what happens means I can support you better, and that's all I want. All Nicti wants. Is there a reason you don't want our help?"

Cambre wanted to cry. Accepting help was admitting something was wrong. Admitting something was wrong was the end of their life.

"I want to stay on the *Sunspot*."

The doctor takes Cambre's hands. "I'm giving you that chance. In case you skimmed the last HR training, and I wouldn't blame you, they've softened their medical requirements. All you need to prove is that you can contribute to keeping this ship running, even if it's not your original job."

He squeezes Cambre's hands gently, and Cambre wonders if the lilian can feel how Cambre's hands are trembling.

"Cambre, without help, you *will* be asked to leave eventually. But needing help doesn't mean you can't stay. It doesn't mean you can't contribute to the small neighborhood we have here in the stars. Please, let me try to find out what's going on."

"So if, if I need, need help walking, I don't have to leave?"

"Of course not. There are so many people on this ship who are not in peak physical condition. Not even the *Sunspot* is without her trouble points. If you need something to help you walk, like a cane, I can get that for you without medically terminating your employment."

Cambre blinked, refusing to cry. They hunched over, clutching the doctor's hands. They'd been so certain admitting they couldn't do their job, declaring that they needed help, meant they'd have to leave their home. But maybe using a cane would give them more energy. Maybe painkillers would let them sleep at night. Maybe something else could settle their stomach, and Cambre could go back to eating their favorite foods across the table from Nicti.

"Okay," they said. "Okay. Let's figure this out."

"Thank you," the doctor said. "Let's talk about things that would make life easier in additional to painkillers and a cane."

Wet In Emergency

"What's in there?" Lernia asks, pointing to a small wall box on her tour of the belly of the cargo ship.

The quartermaster pauses, glancing between the box and her. "I thought you said you'd sailed on a ship before."

"I, um…" Lernia stammers. She has sailed on a ship before, but nothing ocean-going. Nothing as massive as this.

The quartermaster, who is one of her bosses now so Lernia really should learn his name, marches her over to the box. It sticks out and is painted a bright white, easy to see against the ship's grey walls. It's sealed with wax and marked with a pictograph of a whale surrounded by a ring of runes.

"Ship safety rule number four," the quartermaster says. "Never release the whale."

"The whale."

"You are now serving on a ship that goes a month without seeing land. That might go two before we see another ship. We don't use messenger birds - they'd tire before reaching their home base - and there's no guarantee that a flare - magic or other-wise - would be seen before we sink if we run into trouble. We are alone out here, and the likelihood that we come across some sort of trouble our two sea witches can't solve in the next year is high."

He taps the box. "This is our emergency whale. Dehydrated. Asleep. Shrunk. Drop it in the sea and the spells will dissolve, giving us a trained whale big enough to push us to port. But if you release the whale in the hallway. If it accidentally gets wet…"

Lernia swallows. She's pretty sure what would happen was a whale filling up the cargo bay - doing damage to itself and the ship.

"I won't release the whale," she promises.

"Good." The quartermaster shakes his head as he continues with her orientation tour. "Last time I skip an interview," he mutters under his breath.

The Letter Thief

"Burn this," Lady Francis said, holding out a letter as she breezed into the library.

Susan took it with a slight bow, stuffing the folded paper into her apron pocket, barely interrupting her dusting of the shelves. From the corner of her eye, she watched her sit in a chair and open a novel.

At least, she assumed it was a novel. Ladies usually read novels. The rate at which Lady Francis flipped the pages indicated it was not a book full of knowledge to digest.

Susan withheld a sigh, aligning the books on the walnut shelves with a cloth-covered hand as she finished her chore. Susan didn't dare touch one – the bumpy leather covers, the gold embossed letters – because she knew she wouldn't be able to resist slipping a book into her apron pocket and Lady Francis or her husband would certainly notice its absence. But letters to be burned? Well. No one would know if Susan didn't feed them to the fire.

The letter sat in her apron pocket all day, Susan patting the space to ensure she hadn't lost it every time she switched chores.

She only pulled the cream paper out when she got home, sitting on her bed in her shared room at the boarding house. Amelia, her roommate, watched her in the vanity mirror as she washed her face. Amelia also worked as a maid for a wealthy family in the city. Based on the soot she scrubbed off, that day's tasks had been fireplace cleaning.

"Did you steal a letter again?"

"It's not stealing if they're not wanted."

"One day, someone is going to find your collection of scraps. It won't matter that you can't read, they'll believe you took them for some nefarious purpose."

Susan spread the letter on her knees, tracing the black ink with her index finger. The greeting at the top, the paragraphs flowing down the cream paper, the departure at the end. A name, signed with a flourish.

Lady Francis allowed Susan to handle her papers because she was illiterate. Susan had reached New York City by asking for directions, but that wasn't uncommon in the rural parts of Connecticut she had lived in. It was rare for a woman in her town to know how to sign her name. What was the point? What did she need to read? She knew where all the shops were and there was no one she wished to write letters to.

She didn't need to read in the city either, but it would make things easier - reading the labels in shops or the names in windows. She could get the news from the paper, not wait to have someone tell her what it said.

"I'll read someday." Susan slipped her newest letter into a basket near her bed. Her collection was growing, filling half the wicker basket.

"Well, staring at those paper scraps every night is not going to make the knowledge appear in your head."

"You never know." Susan slipped out of her work clothes, careful not to step on the hem. The fabric was thin enough that if she did, the resulting rip might be too large to mend.

Amelia sighed, digging into her trunk for her sleep shift. "Reading isn't proper for women, Susan."

"One day, I'll memorize my entire collection. Every word. Every drop of ink."

"You better stop pilfering then. The more you collect, the more you'll have to memorize."

Susan hadn't considered that, but the next time something to burn crossed her hands, the children's letter practice sheets, Susan pocketed them.

Aphrodite's Feathers

When I open my door to my mother's knocks, she holds up a wooden cage. Her dark curls are starting to fall out of her head scarf, and her gaze bores into me. "You'll use her," she commands, firmly pushing the cage at me.

I take it gently, the dove inside flapping her wings for balance. She's small, but it's probably for the best. The cage is small too.

"Máma,"

"I spent money on that bird, Cora. Keep her."

I sigh. Arguing would get me nowhere. "Did you want coffee?"

She must have understood I offered only due to politeness because she quickly gives an excuse. She frequently comes to gossip after visiting the market; I must have hidden my distaste for the gifted dove poorly. As my mother heads back to her home, I introduce the dove to mine. She's white with kind eyes. She does nothing but coo, and when I hang her from the rafters she doesn't mind the lack of attention I give her.

I expected a creature of Aphrodite to be pushier.

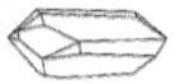

Animals sacred to the love goddess attract love. It's why young girls in the village weave dove feathers into their hair to draw a suiter.

I don't want to use my new dove for anything other than ambient noise, a soft coo to join the wind that sometimes twists through the hills.

But I also don't want to be alone. I want what Máma and Babá have. I remember watching him tease her when I was a child. Her anxiously waiting outside our home for him to return from the fields. Máma visited me last week with a wildflower in her hair, three days wilted but still treasured because Babá had brought it for her.

I want the happiness I can see in her eyes when she looks at my father.

And she wants it for me, enough to spend the money on a whole dove.

I sigh as I work, making neat little stitches as I embroider a waistcoat in the sun streaming in from the window. Simply having a dove in my home is sure to draw a man to my small house.

No man has knocked on my door. Not unless you count little Auggie, who at seven likes to watch my hands. He's a calm, focused child. A reprieve from the other boys in town who run through the streets, kicking a ball between them.

I want to talk to his mother, ask if once she had woven dove feathers in her hair and if so, how long it took for them to draw in her husband. Is a dove a stronger magnet, made of multiple feathers with a live, beating heart? Do my walls block her efficiency? Would I have better luck wandering the village with a feather in my hair?

I have to deliver the embroidered vest to Kostas tomorrow. It's a good time to try.

Besides, if I walk through the village without a feather, Máma will hear of it.

Catching the dove the next morning isn't hard, but we both cry during the process. She flaps, wing bones strong enough to bruise, but in the end, the cage is too small for her to move much. I grab feathers from her tail and yank. I let her cower in the corner, beads of blood on her skin, as I rehang her cage. I brush the three feathers with a soft cloth, smoothing the barbs and cleaning the tips. Then I wipe away my tears, add a feather to the twist of my curls, and stuff the other two in my pocket before picking up Kostas's wrapped embroidered vest.

Kostas runs the bakery across with his wife and two sons, one of whom is unmarried. We haven't interacted much, a consequence of luck versus any other, but maybe today is the day. Maybe Aphrodite will lead Kostas's son's feet to me, my chosen lover.

I walk across the village with my head down, watching for rocks, and imagine my future. A husband at my side, praising my work. Someone to wrap me in a shawl at the end of the day. Who comes home eager to see me. I can't imagine children, but the warmth of a shared home is alluring.

Yet as I approach Kostas's home my feet slow. I would love my dove feathers to guide me to my love, or draw them to me. I want this work, even as I send a prayer to Aphrodite to not let Kostas's son be home.

I want what Máma has so bad, but now that the opportunity is close I find myself shying away.

I deliver the vest and Kostas makes a scene of admiring my grape vine motif. A few villagers smile at his voice, and some look at me, but no one approaches or lingers.

Kostas reaches for the feather tucked into my hair. "Finally trying, koukla?"

I laugh. "I was always looking, but Máma decided it was time for Aphrodite to help."

"Pity my boys aren't home. The feather must not be calling to them."

I smile, face suddenly tight. I want the feather to call someone. I'm glad it has not.

"It's a beautiful day, koukla. Enjoy the sun. Maybe pray to more than just the old gods. You're not getting younger."

I grit my teeth and smile. "If you pay me the remainder, I'll head straight to the church."

He laughs, pulling out his wallet. "You'll run a tight home, Cora."

I take his money and flee.

It doesn't take long to get to the church. I don't go inside, if my mother's prayers haven't worked yet I don't think kneeling in the nave would make a difference. Instead, I wander the town, the dove's feathers on display. I know it's just superstition based on old myths, but so many here believe in them. Almost more so than the words of the Orthodox priest.

Every maiden tucks feathers in her hair. Every young man tucks one in a buttonhole or pocket.

Everyone wants love, and Aphrodite promises that in a way Christianity cannot.

My feet start to ache as I make a point to walk every street, up and down the hills of the village. I run into Eleni, who giggles when she sees the feather in my hair and tells me she only wore hers for a week before Spiros came knocking. Other women smile knowingly when they see me, including Theia Eva who better report back to Máma I'm putting her dove to good us.

I keep my eyes open and my head up, watching for men to turn toward me even as I tense every time they do.

No suitor approaches. I cannot tell if I'm grateful or disappointed.

"You might be in use for a while," I tell the dove when I get home.

She looks at me with baleful eyes, huddled in the same corner of the cage she retreated to this morning. She must still be hurt from this morning, for she doesn't coo. I leave her be.

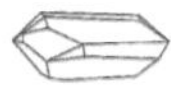

Máma visits a few days later. It's her weekly visit to share the gossip from the next town over. It's only after I pour the coffee from the briki does she ask, "Have you been wearing feathers?"

"Yes, Máma," I say, handing over a cup. "Every time I leave the house." Which has only been thrice since her gift, but the village is only so big. There are only so many bachelors.

"Anyone approached you?"

"No." The coffee is too hot to drink, so I mimic a sip to prevent myself from saying more. Mama likes to pry for details.

Thiea Eva has probably shared them anyway. How I've ambled narrow paths of the village several times now, waiting for the symbol of Aphrodite's creature to guide love to me. How I always walk alone.

"Well," she sighs, "Maybe your love isn't from the village. Keep wearing them, and put the dove closer to the door. Your love may be a traveler."

I'm glad she doesn't recommend I visit the city. It would take over a day to get to it by cart, such a hassle for a half-felt hope.

"The weather is getting nicer. I can hang the dove near the window."

Máma leaves an hour later, kissing my cheek before threatening the dove even as she mutters a blessing to Aphrodite under her breath. I appreciate her dedication to my future happiness.

Half the village women insist my love is beyond the our modest collection of homes. I visit various markets to gain more embroidery clients or sell pieces I made – crochet lace dollies, aprons hems displaying myrtle, handkerchiefs with grape leaves on the edge. I build personalities for the young men I see at the market, but tense every time they approach. I move the dove feathers from my hair to my pocket.

Everyone in my village knows I am looking for love, but most market goers do not know my face or my plight. No woman glances coyly at the white in my hair. No parents nudge their sons my way.

"No luck again?" Kostas asks. Every other week we attend a large market three hours away, one I only sell at because he offers me transport. His cart has been emptied of bread, but filled with flour and eggs. My own basket is lighter, having sold various pieces of lace. I've also received a wedding dress to embroider, carefully wrapped to avoid snagging on the willow wood.

"No luck," I say, leaning against a stack of flour bags. "But I'm beginning to think that is my luck."

He turns around on the seat briefly to look at me, trusting his donkey to follow the road. "You'll find love, koukla. Maybe if you eat your dove, swallow the essence of Aphrodite, men will flock to you like they do her."

"Maybe."

Plucking feathers is distressful enough, I cannot imagine killing my dove.

Kostas reassures me several times on the ride home, but as the sun sets we quiet. I think in the dark about how relieved I am every time a man doesn't pause at my wares. How when a knock on my door doesn't reveal a bashful potential suiter I release my breath. How the only men who have talked to me since I received Máma's gift have been like Kostas – already claimed.

I think it might be possible my feathers aren't drawing in suitors, but pushing away potentials men. Aphrodite will not grant me love.

Because, deep down, she knows I do not want it.

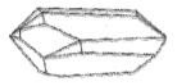

I have dinner with Kostas's family, his wife insists, and I smile at their dynamic. He showers her in kisses and praises her food, she blushes and swats him with a towel. Their children pay no attention to it, but I watch.

There's something soft and nice about being part of a family unit. I know why Máma wants me to have one, and I think I'd like one too. But I'd like a lover in the same way I imagined joining Artemis's group of handmaidens as a child. It's a fantasy.

One I never believed would come true.

I don't need a lover to come home to. I don't need children to fuss over. I tense at the possibility of romance and relax when it disappears. Dove feathers don't work for me, because I don't want that type of love.

I still want it. I want the love Máma showers me with, care and concerns for my future. I adore how Kostas loves me, a friend who supports my craft and shares his family. And all that love means I'll never be truly alone. I'll have customers and dinner with friends and coffee with family. I'll have a life, maybe not the one I imagined nor the one Máma wants me to have, but it's the one that makes me happy. A life that I love.

When I get home, I remove the feathers from my apron pocket and slip them into the dove's cage. I stare at the dove, who sits content in her cage. She glows a soft grey in the moonlight and coos. I coo back and leave the cade door open. I don't need her feathers, and I don't care about my mother's cries when she realizes I've stopped looking for a suiter.

Sometime during the night, the dove leaves. I wake to a small brown hunting dog near my feet, a white crescent over her heart. Aphrodite's dove has abandoned me, I do not need it, but the goddess of love must have mentioned me to to her grand-niece who sent me a more permanent companion better aligned to my life. I scratch the hound's head as I get up, already thinking of the wedding dress I'll embroider for my new client.

I'll never wear one myself, but that's okay.

Intrusive Thoughts

T ouch the train.

Mind reading means Hhitsh knows what a train is. The giant monstrosity coming at them. It's not full speed, but still dangerously fast.

Touch it.

He eyes the woman whose mind he's in. She shoves her hands under her armpits, staring at the ground.

Touch it! Reach out a hand.

"The next train is an inbound express, and will not stop," a voice in the air says. "Please stay behind the yellow line."

Hhitsh should stay behind the yellow line. The train is large. Silver. Dangerous.

Touch the train! Imagine the sleek metal under your hand! Have you ever touched one? You should. You want to.

The woman hunches further into her spine. Hhitsh doesn't understand. How could she think such things, and then not act on them?

The train *would* be smooth. He *hadn't* ever touched one. He *wants* to.

He sticks out his hand.

The train hits it with enough force he nearly loses his hand. It isn't smooth, but rough from all the handles and rivets. He screams, curling around the mangled limb. The people around him shriek as they step back and push forward.

One of those who approach is the woman whose mind he is still reading. No longer does she think about touching trains, but rather her relief that she hadn't. That she knew this would have been the result.

And Hhitsh had known too. It'd been in the back of the woman's mind, and so his as well. But the thoughts had been so loud, so insistent.

"Why didn't you touch the train?" he bites out. "You wanted to."

"You can't obey every little thought that pops into your head." She unwinds her scarf to wrap around his hand, ignoring the shimmer in his blood. She thinks about her uncompleted nursing degree, pressure and elevation. *The arm should be above his heart.*

Hhitsh automatically lifts his arm.

Because he *can't* ignore thoughts. Not a single member of his people can. Thoughts are commands. Guidance. He reads the thoughts of those around him, who read the thoughts of those around them, the entire planet sharing the thoughts of their queen.

Earth has too many minds. Too many dangers.

You're a useless nurse. Look at him sobbing. You're awful. Just awful.

The woman shakes her head, curly hair flying.

Hhitsh suspects he'll kill himself before he can make his first report.

Wrong Guess

"**H**ey, sunshine. You don't have to use that anymore."

Mary ignored the man leaning against the wooden drawers other than a quick flick to his shoes. Shiny. She continued to flip through the cards in the P drawer, bypassing chunks of cardstock on her way to Ptolemy.

The man scooted closer, no longer on the side of the card catalog but leaning against some of the drawers Mary didn't need. From the corner of her eye, she caught sight of burnt orange slacks as she continued toward the back of the drawer.

"I said you don't have to use that anymore. The library has a computer lookup system."

He was closer now. The faint scent of cigarettes hit her nose, and Mary did her best to not breathe it in, even if it smelt better than the marijuana pockets around campus.

"I said –"

"I don't trust the computer system," Mary said stiffly. Her fingers found the edge of a promising card before she looked up at the man. His hair was combed and his face cute, hovering over a fashion-able satin shirt, but his attitude killed any type of attraction.

"You just don't know how to use it, let me show you."

Gently, he pushed the long drawer closed. Mary flicked out her card and pocketed it in her jeans. She cast her eyes around the library, hoping for someone to step up and distract the man, but no one was around.

"You don't need to," she protested as he pulled on her wrist gently.

"I insist."

Grudgingly, she followed.

Only one computer in the library hosted the dig-ital card catalog, and he led her right to it.

"I'm Jack, by the way. Who are you?"

"June," she said.

"And don't you look pretty as spring." He flicked the extra fabric of her peasant top.

Mary sent him a tight smile, but he either didn't notice her unwillingness to be with him or didn't care. Like a gentleman, he offered her a chair at the computer catalog but proceeded to search for her instead of showing her how to use the MARC system.

"What are you looking for?" he asked, opening the program.

"Works on Ptolemy. He's –"

"Famous for his contributions to mathematics." Jack frowned at her. "Are you sure you want to learn about him? The Greeks are great people to learn from, but a babe like you should be more interested in the myths."

Mary straightened her shoulders. "I'm a student at this university looking to write a paper, not a silly girl looking for an evening read."

"Snaps, June."

Mary watched him struggle to spell Ptolemy, but kept her mouth shut, enjoying his increasing frustration at the computer. You'd think a fellow student would have better spelling.

Eventually, he got it right, and several books populated the screen.

"See?" Jack said. "This is all the books the library has on Ptolemy. Title, subtitle, publication, and classification number."

She watched him write down the Dewy Decimal details from the list, scanning the screen. It was the same results she'd gotten when she searched twenty minutes ago.

"And now," Jack stood, offering his hand and out of politeness Mary took it. "We boogie through the stacks to find them! They have similar numbers and will be on the same shelf."

Jack led the way, looking over his shoulder regularly to ensure Mary was following. He asked questions: What was she studying? How did she spend her time? Where did she live? Mary offered a lie or spoke so generally Jack would never be able to find her. He did not know how to retrieve information from computers or people.

Not that computers were smart. The university recently installed so many of them, but Mary found them useless. It was harder to find the information she needed than expected.

"Here we are!" Jack waved a hand at the shelf full of math books. "All the library has on Ptolemy."

"You know why I don't trust the computer, Jack?"

"There's no reason not to, June. Look at-"

"It's because, like the men on campus apparently, they're full of the wrong expectations." Mary flashed the card from the catalog she'd managed to snag before Jack pulled her away. "I'm not looking for Ptolemy, the mathematician. I'm looking for Ptolemy, the Pharaoh of Egypt because I'm a history major. You turkey."

She turned on her heel and marched toward the correct section of the library.

Birthday Bakes

Julie opened the oven door, cursing at the cupcakes. The centers were sunken, even as the edges had taken on a color similar to her wooden cutting board.

Alone in her apartment, she let the tears fall.

"I don't understand," she whispered. "I followed the recipe."

She'd followed the recipe twice, and had no more eggs for a third attempt. She shut the oven door, brushing a mitt-clad hand across her cheek to catch the tears. She needed to bake *something*.

Elsa's birthday was today. Beautiful Elsa, who loved to brush Julie's hair and place her hands on Julie's waist and marvel at her barely-there hourglass figure. Who would stare hungrily as Julie put on makeup and take advantage of her skirts. Wonderful Elsa, who so adored Julie's femininity. Who praised it, appreciated it, loved it.

Julie loved being a woman for Elsa, she really, *really* did. It's just, being a woman was so new. It was easy to lean into the fashion. Grow out her hair, find waisted dresses, padded bras, jewels for her neck. Looking like a woman was easy.

Julie's mom had taught her how to do laundry. She'd learned how to cook edible dishes in college. But bake? A layered cake? From scratch? She was out of her depth.

She pulled out the dozen cupcakes. She thought these would be easier. Just pour the cake batter from the recipe into a different shape, and she only needed one good cupcake to present as a birthday surprise.

Despondent, Julie grabbed a handful of toothpicks and started poking the cupcake centers. The book said a fully baked cake would leave the toothpick clean. None of her pokes were.

She shoved the tray out of the way and leaned over the kitchen counter, forearms on the sticky linoleum and forehead pressing against her thumbs.

She'd followed the instructions. She wasted so many ingredients. Elsa would be home soon. Julie had to start dinner; birthday dessert would be the frost-bitten ice cream in the freezer.

The first tear dripped down her face to land on the kitchen counter. A dozen more quickly followed until Julie was outright sobbing. She turned and slid down to the floor, cabinet handles digging into her back as the lingering heat from the oven warmed her right side.

Julie cried until she heard the click of the lock.

She scrambled to her feet, glancing at the oven clock. The kitchen was a mess; half-cooked, half-burnt cupcakes cooling in the tray on the burners, charred rounds in layer cake pans shoved near the air fryer, flour dusting the floor. She'd wanted Elsa to come home to a clean house, dinner cooking, and something frosted on display.

Not, not this.

"Julie?"

Elsa dropped keys in the bowl and rushed over, not bothering to take off her shoes. Her hands cradled Julie's strong jaw, brushing away the tears that had started anew.

"What's wrong, babe?"

"I, I wanted to be a good wife for you," Julie hiccupped. "I tried to bake a cake, but I-" She fell forward, head landing on Elsa's shorter shoulder. "I'm sorry. I'm a failure. I'm sorry."

Elsa cooed, gently guiding Julie off the floor to sit at the kitchen table. Elsa crouched next to it, keeping their faces level.

"You didn't fail. I see a dozen cupcakes right there."

"The center is raw."

Elsa carded fingers through Julie's hair, making soothing noises until Julie's cry finished.

"I'm very happy you wanted to make me something for my birthday."

"But I didn't," Julie repeated. She turned her head, staring at the kitchen mess.

"Doesn't matter."

"But it does!"

"Can you tell me why?"

"I wanted to do something special for your birthday," she muttered. "And I wanted to do something femme."

"And baking is femme?"

Julie peeled away. The loss of Elsa's fingers made her want to keen, but Julie swallowed it down. "I want to be a woman."

"You are a woman-"

"I want to be a woman," Julie said again, ignoring Elsa's disruption. "I like being one. And you like me when I'm femme. And baking is what women do."

"Maybe in the past." Elsa took her hand. "Have you ever seen me bake?"

"You do cookies."

"I do Pillsbury cookies. I slice the dough and turn on the oven. That's not baking." Elsa sighed. "Look, you know you'll never exactly look like the women you stare at, yeah?"

Julie nodded. Hormones were far away – the far side of therapy and good insurance and a nest egg she wasn't sure she could build. But she had done her best with what she could – her narrow, thin body easy to transform. In the mirror, her Adam's apple felt obvious, but most people ignored it.

"I don't have to look like them," Julie said, a statement her therapist has mostly drilled into her head. "It's more important that I look a way that makes me happy."

Elsa rubbed her thumb over the back of Julie's hand. "Right. Each woman is unique. And just because I also have long hair and am currently in a dress, would you call me femme? Based on the conventional standard."

Julie shook her head. They'd met in a gym after all, Julie watching as Elsa deadlifted a hundred pounds, biceps straining and thighs tight in spandex.

"If you want to bake, bake, but don't do it because you think you need to. Or that I want you to. Okay?"

Julie nodded. "Okay," she whispered.

Elsa leaned in for a quick kiss and Julie let her.

"I'm gonna have a cupcake," Elsa announced.

"Don't, please! You'll get sick."

Elsa slid out of her grasp and over to the cupcakes. She plucked one from the center of the tray, peeled back the yellow paper, and took a bite. Julie watched in horror and love as Elsa tried to hide her disgust.

Elsa swallowed thickly. "Okay," she said. "If you really want to learn how to bake, I'll set up time with my mom to teach us."

Julie laughed, joining her wife in the kitchen. She wrapped her arms around Elsa, softly laughing. "I told you."

"I wanted to taste it. But please, if you bake again, make sure it tastes better."

"Sorry, I ruined your birthday."

Elsa kissed her temple. "You showed me you care and love me, and that's all I need."

"Sap."

"Guilty."

"Let me clean up, and then let's go out. I don't want to be in the kitchen longer than I need to."

"A romantic candlelight dinner for my birthday?"

"My treat, complete with cake I didn't bake."

Julie kissed Elsa properly, hands tangled in hair.

"We could still eat the frosting later," Elsa whispered in Julie's ear.

Well, at least not all of Julie's baking supplies would go to waste.

The Goddess Of Modern Marriage

You press your hands to your face, hiding your eyes. You know it's Hera before you, but as the goddess of marriage she's taken on the form of your ideal wife, *your* wife. It's hard to hear a woman who looks and sounds like Nikoleta say to your face she wants a divorce.

"I'm not sure I'm the lawyer for you, my Hera. Surely there's a single man who can help you better?"

"Spiros," Hera says, and her voice is Nikoleta's high alto, the voice she uses when she's placing dinner on the table and serving in the bedroom, "I need a husband to represent me. And I know Athenian law doesn't apply to Olympians, so don't make that argument either."

By the end, her voice is different and her face is wrinkled. Not Nikoleta, but your mother Evyenia and she's smiling with the doting look she'd give her husband Dimitri every time he brought her a shawl.

"I need you to be my lawyer because you are everything Zeus is not. You are a kind and loyal husband. You make Nikoleta meals and take the children to the park. And when the chance came for you to cheat, you chose not to."

You blush, remembering the looks of your boss's secretary as she led you to meetings. The slide of a phone number across the counter of your regular lunch spot.

"My divorce from Zeus is simply a side effect of what I'm trying to do, and you're perfect for the job, Spiros. I promise."

"And what are you trying to do?"

"I'm the Goddess of Marriage, certainly that means I should represent its current expression. Embody a healthy balance of work and vulnerability and showcase that you should never, ever feel compelled to stay in a toxic relationship. For some marriages, divorce *is* the right answer. So I'll lead by example, divorce my cheating husband, and enter into a new marriage. One that reflects the mutual respect between modern Greek couples. Such as you and Nikoleta."

"Are you saying I'm a better model for a husband than Zeus?"

Hera laughs. "Most people are. But this isn't about Zeus, he will always be king and sky and lightning. Those things are unchanging. Marriage and its practices are a reflection of culture. As they shift, so do I. And who knows?"

She leans back in the chair, form melting from Evyenia to Nikoleta to a stranger, rolling her torso to draw attention to her breasts. "Maybe my next marriage will be to a woman. Those are on the rise. Or perhaps another man, but we declare the marriage open. Maybe...two spouses. One of each. As the Goddess of Marriage, I have to set an example for all who worship me. Weren't you and Nikoleta looking for a third?"

You swallow. "I'll speak to her."

Hera leans forward in her chair, face shifting again to Nikoleta's. "That is why you'll be my lawyer, Spiros. The communication you have with your wife. How all your decisions are joint. Your marriage is, shall I say, the type I wish to represent and encourage my followers to have. We'll see about anything else later."

"I sincerely doubt we'd satisfy you, my Hera."

"You never know." She winks.

Agatha's Curse

You watch as Agatha arranges the thick vine around you in a circle. It's been forty years since she's cursed you, and while you haven't become friends during that time, you have learned more about magic.

Spell circles work like lenses. Wide means more light, or magical energy collection. Close means selectively choosing a target. Agatha leaves barely a hand length between your shoes and the vine.

This spell attempt has something to do with plants as the circle is a vine. It hasn't worked before, but Agatha always has some new idea to break the curse.

Originally, you'd laughed at Agatha's curse. Dying the day you give birth to a child? You have no desire for sex, let alone children. You thought the curse wouldn't stick. Or that it was too weak to take, coming from a skinny witch in training.

But then you got sick. The whole village got sick. Agatha was the closest witch, no longer an apprentice but in full possession of her hat. She arrived at the village just in time to ease the passing of its last residents.

Except you. You hovered on death's door for an hour before recovering. You thanked Agatha for her kindness. She responded by looking you in the eye and asking "Is it a kindness, knowing you're the last one left?"

You didn't answer and Agatha left, onward to respond to some other need. She returned a year later, to a husk of a village holding only you, and you had a response then. "No."

It took some casting to figure out what happened. Agatha's curse, spat out of anger and frustration from a bad day launched toward a laughing spectator, had taken. As it's criteria – giving birth – is something your asexuality balked at, the curse's action – death – is held at bay. You could only die one way, and avoiding it had indirectly granted you immortality. And now that you knew of the curse, you're less inclined to find a partner – you know the pain of being left behind by loved ones.

Agatha returns to the village, now known for being haunted, once a year to try to break the curse. She's given up overpowering it, a circle as wide as the village cast under a full moon hadn't managed to do it. Instead, Agatha keeps trying to alter the wording. Maybe the spell could be convinced your child was an adopted stray cat. Maybe it could be convinced to not be your child, but Agatha's as the caster.

Nothing has worked, and by now Agatha has spawned witchlings. You've met two.

Lately, she's been trying variations of plant parenting. You've adopted the abandoned village gardens and care for dozens of plants in your home.

As you watch, Agatha stands. She places a hand on her back to arch and you hear a soft crack. She's in her sixties now, and contrary to belief she won't live to be over a hundred. Magic is hard on a body. A witch often looks older than she is.

In contrast, you stopped aging the day you were supposed to die with the rest of the village.

You wonder if Agatha has ten more years in her. Ten more chances to break the curse before you're left to be the hermit of a dead village. Perhaps one of her children would try in her stead.

On the vine circle, you notice dead plants. This is new.

"What are the tokens for?"

"I want to try shifting a different word. We've tried 'child', and the possessives."

You nod.

"Now, I want to try 'born'."

"To what?"

She cackles. "'Death.' So that you'd die when your first child dies."

"But I'm lacking a child. We've never been able to convince the spell I have one."

"It might be a matter of timing. The curse is to strike you down at the moment of birth. Anything you've acquired, plants or pets, wasn't yours at the right moment and magic can't off you in the past. I want to try changing it so that when your plants die, you die."

You nod but have low confidence. Oh, Agatha tries, but it's been forty-three years and this would change two parts of the spell when you're not sure Agatha has ever charged one.

Still, the witch chants and lights her tallow and twists the smoke from the burning plants. You feel zero difference.

"How do we test it?"

"Don't water your plants for a few days and we'll see how you feel. I'm old and need recovery time anyway."

Agatha stays for three days. Your garden withers but you don't feel sick. You don't start to die. You resign yourself to another year alone, unable to leave the graves of your family. On the day Agatha prepares to leave, a girl wanders into town.

She is maybe seven, with bleeding feet and a ripped dress. It's fine quality, and you peg her as a survivor of a coup against her noble parents. Small enough to hide. Skinny enough to slip through cracks.

Agatha takes one look at her and beckons her forward. "Looking for a new life, girl?"

"I don't want to learn how to be a witch."

Agatha cackles. "No need. But you need someone, and so does she."

The girl looks at you. You offer her a meal she shyly accepts. Agatha stays another day, watching, and you can see her mind working.

"I want to try a circle again," she says. Why not? Best try as many times as Agatha is willing while she can.

"Girl, come with us."

It's not quite dusk, but the moon is up. She stomps down grass to form a circle as wide as her hips and has you step into it. It's such a crude circle, she can't expect to use it for a spell, can she?

"Girl!" Agatha snaps. "Hold your arms in a circle around her."

Your eyes widen as you watch Agatha position the orphan between yourself and the moon. You stand still as the witch puts a candle in the girl's hand. Pricks your skin and smears the blood on the child. Agatha chants her spell, and you recognize what she's doing. Tying you to the foundling and changing the timing of the curse's activation.

Something ignites in your belly.

It reminds you of when you were cursed. You'd assumed it was a bad cramp at the time, days early, and that same pain hits now. You grunt and Agatha laughs. When the last smoke from the candle fades away you laugh too.

You sweep the girl, your adopted daughter, into your arms and swing her around. She shrieks, confused, and you set her dizzy on her feet. You kiss Agatha on each wrinkly cheek. Tears slip down both of your faces.

"Neither of you will be the last one left. You'll go together," the witch says.

"Thank you," you sob out. For the shifted curse, for her company over the past decades, for the hope granted for the decades to come. "Thank you so much, Agatha."

"Thank you, Marylynn, for letting me help you."

Three Raindrops

On rainy full moons, I line my yard with buckets to catch the water. I cork it in bottles and keep them in a cool place. When I need soothing, I pour myself of glass to sip the peace of a rainstorm in the dark.

I hold my hand under the roof's edge and watch my palm fill drop by drop. My arm aches while time stretches, but that's the spell's sacrifice. When my palm is full, I bring it to my sister's mouth and watch her pain fade away.

The storm ripples distort the reflection of the moon in the backyard pond. I think I imagine it flash snowdrop-blue. I don't imagine the sudden burst of wings sending pond water rushing over the stones.

Unconditional Love

"Come, cricket."

Ches trotted after her mother as she set out into the woods. She was familiar with its moist soil and humid air, but not enough to navigate the roots crossing the path in the dark. After the third time she tripped, catching her balance while trying to not fall on the fragile lantern, she turned to the vague form of her mother, pale skin covered in dark fabric.

"Can't we light the lantern now?"

"Is this where you want the spirits to find us?"

"No," Ches grumbled.

Her mother laughed. "Let us stand for a moment and get our dark eyes."

Ches fidgeted, shifting her weight from foot to foot. A soft, chilly breeze made the woods creak. Ches looked up; individual branches were hard to see but the stars beyond came into focus. Slowly, she saw more and more stars. Eventually, Ches could distinguish the thin trees around them. Spotting the path was harder, obvious only by the wider gaps between trunks.

"I have my dark eyes now," Ches said.

"Me too, but hold on to my hand, just in case."

Ches squeezed her mother's hand, then they walked into the dark.

Ches's sandal posts sank slightly into the earth, but not enough to make walking hard. The deeper into the woods they traveled, the harder the ground became. The trees got bigger, the size of Ches's whole body, and she stepped closer to her mother's side, careful of the trailing skirt. In paying attention to her feet, she let her arm drop and felt the lantern brush against the dry leaves of a bush.

With a gasp, Ches dropped her mother's hand to pull the wooden frame to her chest, careful of the rice paper sides.

Her mother stopped walking. "If you're tired, or need to concentrate on your footing, I can carry the lantern."

Ches hugged the lantern tighter. It was as large as her head and bulky, but carrying it was an honor and Ches didn't want to give that up. She was ten. She can walk through the woods with a lantern. But it was getting hard holding it high and careful, making sure it didn't bump her knees or a tree. Her arm started to ache.

"How much longer?"

"Only a little bit."

"I can make it."

They continued walking, Ches hugging the lantern. The trees creaked and branches snapped in the wind. Something rustled and Ches stared into the undergrowth, looking for a tail, only to stumble over a rock.

"Careful," her mother said, gripping her shoulder.

"I'm fine. Are we almost there?"

"Look ahead."

With her dark eyes, Ches noticed a thinning of the trees ahead. She rushed forward, pulling to a stop at the edge of a clearing larger than the temple. She had been here before during the day and knew there was a short, wide rock with a flat top in the middle, but at night she couldn't see it from the clearing's edge.

She could see the sky.

"Woooow." She craned her neck back, staring at the stars. Her gaze caught on the thin ribbon of faint stars that stretched up from the southern horizon. She would have toppled if her mother hadn't gently placed a hand on the small of her back.

As she guided Ches upright, her mother took the rope hanging from the lantern's head. Once they stepped into the clearing, they'd be on holy ground. Ches didn't have the blessings necessary to carry the lantern beyond the edge of the woods. She'd only just been able to see the clearing last month.

"Come, Ches."

Her mother strode forward. Ches followed, shaking off the tingle as she crossed into the holy space only those blessed could access. Dead, long grasses brushed her ankles, making them itch. At least her arms were covered; away from the trees, the winter night was sharper. She wouldn't freeze, winter was never dangerous this far south, but she wished for another layer of warmth.

Ches shivered, then spread her arms wide. She twirled, laughing as the stars spun and her skirt swished around her ankles.

"Remember," her mother's voice interrupted her spinning. "We're here for a reason."

Ches scampered forward, reaching her mother's side as she placed the lantern on the center stone. Ches watched as she adjusted it so the lantern door faced the star ribbon. Then, she turned and attacked Ches's clothing.

"We want to give the spirits one last beautiful look at the world, not a disheveled priestess-in-training."

Ches batted her mom's hands away, eager to straighten herself out. As she did so, her lessons surfaced. She had only started training two months ago, but eventually, she'd take over her mother's job of maintaining the town's temple. This rite, happening every first new moon of the year, was the most important thing she would do.

Grey skirt straight, sleeve elbows in place, navy sash across her right shoulder, Ches stood tall.

The temple priestess nodded in approval. Her skirts were longer, trailing through the grass while Ches's came to the top of her ankles. Her sash laid in the opposite direction, and the navy fabric and silver detail made it look like the night sky had wrapped a finger around her torso, mimicking the celestial ribbon behind her, leaving a silver star hair ornament in her dark hair.

Her mother was beautiful.

Ches placed her hands over each other near her thighs and bowed. "I'm ready to begin, Priestess."

"You're here to simply observe. You can ask questions as we walk back."

Ches nodded.

The priestess positioned herself behind the rock altar, blocking Ches's view of the lantern. Then, she sang a song about memory as she circled the rock; how happy memories could keep grief at bay, and how family and friends wished to give the spirits of the dead one last memory to ease their way to the beyond. The lantern began to glow, softly at first as if it held a single glowworm, but gradually grew until it threw shadows in the shape of the names written on the rice paper.

At the end of the song, the priestess faced the lantern and read one of the delicately inked names before performing a series of movements with her head, jerky enough that Ches worried it was a fit until she realized they were calculated to make the tiny bells on her hair ornament sing.

As the soft chimes faded, a ball of light zoomed out of the lantern, silver like the stars. It swirled around the lantern once, then the priestess, and then Ches, who held her breath hoping she was a good last memory for the spirit to take to the sky. A pretty girl, a pretty night, a pretty voice, and knowledge that while dead, they will not be forgotten.

"Remember us as we remember you," the priestess sang and the bead of starlight, the soul of the person whose name she had read, raced to the sky, following the thin trail of faint stars to the horizon.

Ches watched diligently as her mother read all seven names on the lantern, the black ink disappearing with each new soul leaving. Ches tried to follow each up into the sky, but they quickly became just another star in the vast expanse above her.

As the seventh soul left to rise above the Earth, Ches turned her attention to her mother with a dozen questions on her tongue. They died when she saw the lantern was still lit.

Ches had walked through town with her mother yesterday, collecting the names of those who died the past year. She watched as someone close to the deceased painted the names on rice paper, too delicate for pens. Seven names collected, seven names written, seven names spoken.

Seven souls to send to the sky.

There was an eighth glowing in the lantern.

Ches didn't know what to do; her mother had told her to watch, not participate. She wasn't trained to do the rite. She didn't have a starclad sash, just a regular navy one. She had no hair ornaments, no little bells to ring.

And the priestess had no name to speak.

She tried to catch her mother's eye, but she stood on the far side of the rock looking down at the lantern, sadness on her face.

Wind rushed through the clearing and Ches bit her lip to prevent a shiver. The soul dimmed, then flared and began to sing.

I came when called by memory, a sweet voice singing of the sadness of loss even as they sang of the joy of having known me and treasuring those moments. I came when called by a promise, to hear my name one last time and witness the beauty of this world one last night. I waited to be called, but I am still here! I am forgotten!

The soul sounded sad and young, voice wailing on the last word as the lantern flickered. The light turned from a warm glow to an angry one, flashing red. The priestess stepped back seconds before flames started to consume the rice paper, now empty of names.

Forgotten! Unknown!

The soul reminded Ches of an infant who only knew how to scream and she remembered talking with her friend Paloti that afternoon. She'd been so excited because her little brother or sister would be there soon.

"I haven't met them yet, but I already love them," Paloti said, wrapping her hands around herself.

Hearing the news had made Ches happy because when she had gone around town with her mother the evening before collecting names, Paloti's father had been nervous.

"Don't go making the bad happen," he had pleaded, twisting a rag while staring at a silhouette of his wife passing by a window, belly round and another woman helping her walk. He hadn't written a name for the lantern. Hadn't whispered one in the priestess's ear.

Paloti's joy earlier made Ches think everything was fine. The baby should have been born tonight, placed in Paloti's arms and rocked while Ches walked the woods with her mother.

Unloved! The soul shrieked.

Ches remembered Paloti's bright, eager smile.

"Noo~." Ches didn't know what she was doing, but she knew that you had to sing. She drew out the word, going up in pitch.

The priestess's eyes were wide, warning her to be careful, but Ches continued. The flames on the lantern paused, rice paper almost eaten. If the flames moved to the dead grass, the clearing would burn in minutes.

"You are the sibling of Paloti, who told me this morning she loved you. She would kiss you inside your mom."

The flames shrunk and the soul stopped wailing.

The priestess took over, her strong alto overpowering Ches's reedy voice. "You are the child of Sonra, who sang to you of her love. The child of Tovas, who whispered endearments to you every night. You were unnamed, but not unloved. You have no name because you were not here long enough for it to be called. You were loved regardless, and we offer this last beautiful view of the world before you depart for the stars."

The soul cried, but softer as the flames extinguished.

"Remember us as we remember you," the priestess sang, moving her head to tinkle the bells in a call for the soul to witness the night.

The soul left the lantern. It slowly circled the rock, doing an extra loop around the priestess and Ches before zooming toward the sky.

Ches tracked the soul until it was just another point of starlight.

"Oh dear." Her mother crouched to inspect the lantern. "We'll have to build a new frame for next year."

She spoke it, not sang, and Ches relaxed knowing the rite was over. She rushed toward her mother, wrapping her arms around her waist while peering at the lantern. Ashes rung its place on the rock, the remnants of rice paper. While it was too dark to see where the wood turned to charcoal, Ches noticed thin spots where the flames had eaten the frame.

Her mother stroked her hair. "You did well, Ches. You remembered to sing, and knew what to say to calm the child."

Ches smiled, proud, before deflating. "This means Paloti didn't get a baby sister. She really wanted one."

Her mother leaned down to kiss the crown of her head. "We'll visit the family tomorrow and tell them we're sorry. You can give Paloti a big, big hug and tell her something important."

"What's that?"

"That the baby followed the other villagers into the land of the gods, and left knowing it was loved."

Her mother blew away the ashes before gathering up the lantern. "Come, cricket. I have my dark eyes again and it's late. Let's walk home and get to bed." She held out her hand.

Ches took it, reaching for the lantern for the other.

"You sure? It got heavy for you on the way here."

"Yes."

She'd always known the rites were important, but now that Ches had seen it performed, heard the voices of the souls of those the village lost, she wanted to do everything she could. She wanted to tell Paloti she did her best and tell her friend's family that Ches would always be there for them – as Paloti's best friend and as the future village priestess.

Ches's mother passed over the lantern, the rope through its head miraculously intact. "Mind the roots."

Holding hands, they entered the trees and headed home.

Rowdy Children

Lucifer crouches in front of the child. He's young and covered in snot, all that's left from an hour of pleading. There's no blood, at least, though Lucifer knows on Earth the child had to be surrounded by quite a lot.

By rights, the kid should be in Heaven. Innocent soul, and all that. Too young for any sin. But cults have a way of unbalancing the natural order, and this one has figured out a way to separate a soul from its body and send it ahead to a designated place. Hell, in this case. Hoping that such a gift would be pleasing and be returned in kind.

Lucifer has no such plans.

"Do you know why you're here?" He asks, holding out a soft bit of cloth. The child flinches from his claws but allows Lucifer to clean his face.

"I asked too many questions," the boy hiccups, unable to look away from Lucifer's skin.

Lucifer frowns. Children are curious creatures. They learn by playing or questions, but he has seen too many parents treating their child's curiosity as something to ignore. Like snapping at a dog barking at the postman, some people will yell at kids for the smallest inconvenience. Children to them are craft projects, things they created, but then wish would disappear because they take up too much space. But while you can toss that painting from last year's wine-and-paint night, you cannot toss a child.

Unless you're in the right cult.

Lucifer pulls back the cloth, cataloging the boy's face. Blond curls. Grey eyes. Thin.

"My mom said I asked too many questions too."

The boy looks up at that and Lucifer doesn't hide what he is. Jagged horns on his head, leathery wings, skin so pink it looks like a sunburn. He stares at the boy, and the boy stares back.

"I still annoy my mom," Lucifer says. "Do you want to bother yours?"

The boy looks at his lap. "I'm supposed to leave her alone."

"Children aren't meant to be peaceful. We're chaotic and full of questions. I'll show you my favorite tricks to annoy moms if you want?"

Lucifer stretches out his hand, claws out. After a moment, the boy gently places his hand on Lucifer's, little fingers cool on the devil's hot skin. Lucifer knows that he'll be a much better parent.

Etched in Brass

The shop bells chimed. Jackson looked up from the counter where he'd been polishing machine parts. The woman who entered wore simple pieces that were neat and clean, but a few seasons old. He frowned as he watched her look at the instruments in the window and display cases on the walls. If she could afford any of them, Jackson would eat a boot.

"Hello, sir."

Jackson placed down the gear and straightened. He rarely got called sir, he was just a shop assistant as his uncle loved to remind him, but he fully planned on taking control of the perceived status of being an experienced occultist.

"Morning, ma'am. How can I assist you?"

"I heard you sell devices that can protect a person or place."

"Indeed we do."

She clasped her hands together. Her gloves lacked lace. Still, if Uncle Jonathan knew he didn't give a customer proper respect, he'd be yelled at.

"What type of protection do you need?"

"I'm cursed and would like it removed."

Jackson raised an eyebrow. "Can I have more detail?"

"I'm a private vocal instructor, and teach several young ladies in town. However, many of them are getting sick and I believe me, or rather my curse, is the reason why."

"Ma'am, there are many reasons why someone may get sick-"

"Every single one of my pupils? Ten young ladies across the city?"

Jackson sighed. Everyone believed the supernatural was the reason for their troubles even if it was illogical. But his uncle had built a reputation – every problem heard. For his uncle to truly teach Jackson how to be an occultist, not just run the shop, he had to uphold the same standards.

Listen. Offer a solution.

Maybe, make a sale. With no guarantee it would work. They couldn't know the rules *every* spirit operated by after all.

"I'll call for tea," Jackson said, gesturing to a small table in the corner. It'd allow him to watch for other patrons while listening to the tutor's troubles but provided a more proper location to have a conversation than a counter filled with grease, dirty rags, and cuts of metal.

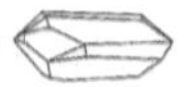

The music tutor was Ms. Emily Farthington, and the more she spoke the more Jackson realized she might truly be cursed. Every young lady she taught developed the same symptoms, and the illness hadn't spread to the household. More damning, further exposure to Ms. Farthington seemed to increase its severity.

First, it was a sore throat, which made an appearance halfway through the lesson. The girl would be recovered by the next lesson, only for the singer's hoarseness to reappear during vocal warmups. The ailment had started to linger for the days between lessons, leading to difficulty breathing, coughs. One student had collapsed as Ms. Farthington knocked on the door to announce her presence.

"A family fired me a three weeks ago," Ms. Farthington said, staring at her empty tea mug. "They feared something about me was making their daughter sick. My perfume, perhaps. Another family informed me that the girl went from struggling to breathe to riding within a week of her last lesson with me. They then told me that by releasing me from their services, they hoped their daughter could make similar progress."

She stared up at Jackson, tears in her lashes. "I lost my fourth client this morning. If I'm to retain my lodgings, I *can't* lose another."

"You feel no illness yourself?" Jackson asked. He racked his mind for which of his uncle's devices might help, but most were preventative. They established wards before a possession or haunting happened.

"None."

"What about in the past?"

"Oh, I've had my share of bad days."

"Anything like what your students have experienced?"

"I," she placed her hand at the base of her neck, the web of her thumb pressing against her collar.

"Ms. Farthington?"

"When I was younger, my sister and I came down with a similar illness. Difficulty speaking, then the coughs, having a hard time getting air. The doctor said something had gotten into our lungs. We were sick for over a month, and she succumbed to it." As she spoke, her hand lowered, rubbing at a spot on her chest.

Jackson watched the movement. It was too below her neck to be in remembered pain. "Are you alright?"

Ms. Farthington blushed as she realized what she was doing. "Oh. My sister was a magpie. She would discover small, shiny objects on the street or shop floors and bring them home. When we were sick, she used a brass disk as a worry talisman. It was one of the few treasures our mother found and gave her. I paid a jeweler to etch her likeness and turn the disk into a necklace years ago. Rubbing it has become a nervous habit."

"Can I see it?"

"I'm afraid there's rather a few layers between my fingers and the clasp." She said stiffly.

He coughed into his hands and scrambled to recover. "Right. Well, I believe that disk may have something to do with your curse. I'd like to run an experiment. Can you bring it back later today?"

She rubbed the same spot, before nodding. "If you think it'll help. I can't afford to lose more students."

"I do."

"I'll come by shortly before you close, if amendable. I'd rather this curse lifted sooner than later."

Jackson twirled the disk in the dim candlelight. Ms. Farthington had given it to him only after he promised not to damage it. He'd also promised to only hold it a single night; the tutor was very attached to the memento of her sister, which meant there was no chance to ask his uncle's advice.

He rolled the chain in his fingers, watching the disk move. The etching on one side was well done, immortalizing a girl of ten. Her resemblance to Ms. Farthington was similar enough Jackson wondered if they were twins. There were occult connections between twins. Not always, but often. Was the spirit pushing back the veil and gripping the throats of young singers, cursing her sister's students?

What would she have against the other girls?

He spun the disk in the other direction and watched the candlelight flash off the one-inch circle. It'd been lovingly taken care of, the brass polished to a high sheen.

Uncle Jonathan used silver frequently in his work as an occultist; the metal reflected the spirits unseen to the bare eyes and it was used for many informational gathering tools. Brass, Jackson knew, had defensive uses. There were several devices in the shop, full of pendulums and searching rods, that emitted a wave designed to keep spirits away. Brass knuckles were able to knock a possessing spirit out of a man. And in the cellar, the dark chamber where his uncle kept ghosts and ghouls he had trapped, were pieces of polished brass in locked wooden boxes.

Jackson watched the disk twist, flipping between the etched portrait and the smooth back. Was the brass charm a defensive tool or a trap for Ms. Farthington's sister? Now that it wasn't around Ms. Farthington's neck, his test was live. Pity it put Ms. Farthington at risk.

Jackson didn't have his uncle's ability with the supernatural, but he was very good at business.

When Ms. Farthington failed to show the next morning to claim her memento, Jackson closed up the shop to pay her a visit. She lent a room at a popular boarding house, so it was no matter to hail a carriage and tell the driver where to go.

Jackson expected two possible results of his test – either Ms. Farthington would get sick, or not. As it turned out, she'd gotten sick quickly. The mistress running the house hesitated to let Jackson see her, but when he mentioned he believed Ms. Farthington cursed and had the means to help, she instructed a maid to take him to the appropriate room.

Watching Ms. Farthington struggle with the same illness her students had caught, he came to two conclusions. One, the disk had not been serving as a trap for the dead sister but as protection for Ms. Farthington. Two, the spirit causing problems was going after Ms. Farthington.

Jackson wasn't a full-fledged occultist. His uncle grudgingly taught him, and he'd never tried understanding a spirit by himself. However, he had witnessed the process multiple times, and the maid peering from the corner had no way of knowing it was his first spiritual diagnosis. With that in mind, he took a deep breath and stepped toward the bed, ignoring the faint smell of sweat.

Jackson pulled out and unwrapped three small silver instruments, arranging them around Ms. Farthington's pillow. His uncle had a knack for reading them in seconds, half science, half intuition. Jackson took longer but got answers he was confident in.

The spirit was family. It wanted revenge. The desire had been present for a while, possibly linked to the deceased sister. There was no other reason the memento was strong enough to reflect the curse for so long.

Jackson turned to the maid. "Did someone in Ms. Farthington's family pass recently?"

She nodded. "Her mother, six months ago."

"Must not have had a good relationship," Jackson muttered.

He padded his pockets, wincing. There was a reason his uncle maintained a packed bag of supplies. Jackson hadn't brought the tools needed to talk to a spirit or any of the blessed items required for banishment.

All he found was a lighter, some tobacco, and the brass disk. He'd have to trap Ms. Farthington's mother within the visage of her daughter.

Jackson looked around for an oil tray, but the boarding house had traded lamps for electric lights. He snagged a tea saucer and hand mirror from the dresser, placing them on opposite sides of the room. Some herbs produced a smoke that clung to spirits, allowing them to be seen. Tobacco wasn't ideal, but it would suffice. He lit the leaves, half in the tea saucer and half on the back of the mirror, lamenting the loss of a good smoke.

Jackson had only seen his uncle trap a spirit a few times. Usually, Jonathan sent a spirit to the world beyond or talked it into leaving – both far easier. He asked the maid to leave and felt relieved when she nodded.

If he failed, no one would know and he could blame Ms. Farthington's death on being there too late. He should have been called early that morning.

Cursing his inability to plan, Jackson hastily went through Ms. Farthington's vanity. He found a brass hat pin, which would do. Now to herd the spirit into the disk.

Jackson watched the smoke swirl, looking for a spot where it stuck and didn't flow with the air currents. An ash cluster appeared hovering over Ms. Farthington's head. Slowly he stepped toward it, brass disk on his outstretched palm. As soon as the disk was under the ash-dusted form, Jackson brought the hat pin down from above as if he were performing an overhand clap.

"Drat," he said, meeting resistance. He'd managed to condense the spirit, trapping it between the hat pin and disk. Jackson struggled to push the pin down, pressing against the air three inches above his palm.

On a whim, Jackson flipped the charm so the portrait of Ms. Farthington's sister faced up. The spirit screeched. Jackson strongarmed the spirit into the brass, slamming the hat pin's shaft onto the disk.

At the supernaturally loud *ding*, Ms. Farthington opened her eyes and gasped.

Jackson quickly arranged his hair and collar before attempting herd the smoke out the window.

"You were right, Ms. Farthington." Jackson picked up the instruments one by one, sliding tobacco ash into the waste basket. "You were cursed by your mother. I imagine she was upset your child-hood illness took you instead of your sister, and saw a chance to remediate that. You'll live, and your students are healed. I'll be taking your etching of your sister though, I had to trap your mother in it."

Ms. Farthington blinked at him. Jackson tugged on his lapels. "The shop will send you a bill for services."

He rushed out to the sound of the maid exclaiming in awe at Ms. Farthington's quick recovery.

Jackson rubbed the brass disk in his pocket. He'd have to show his uncle he was an occultist in his own right, not just an apprentice to mind the shop and polish the inventory.

Addictive Meditation

"We can be like coffee."

"Coffee?" James raised his eyebrow and stared at Stephanie.

She stared at her empty mug, head down on the desk. "Coffee... subscriptions."

James snorted. He looked toward the other end of the boardroom, where the doctor slept. Lingering paranoia meant he'd circled himself with chairs, which was useless. There were guards outside.

"Not following," James said.

They'd been unexpectedly shoved into the room and locked up tight, just like the doctor. It was a little after midnight, but he and Stephanie had pulled all-nighters before, brainstorming on a deadline.

The doctor had some cure for cancer in their head. Or maybe their laptop. And it wasn't just some theory, it was a legitimate threat to the pharmaceutical industry based on the amount of times someone tried to take his life in the past month. A miracle cancer drug that would get rid of hyper-specific drugs, treatments, and procedures to make thousands of bill codes obsolete. Especially if the doctor went through with his plan to release his research for free.

Except someone at Harbor Stix saw profit potential. They'd ordered the doctor kidnapped and secured, and for James and Stephanie to brainstorm a brand-new market strategy to roll out after the treatment was distributed.

"Subscriptions," Stephanie said, "are the money maker. Steady payments versus lump fees. Keep charging for access."

"We sell cigarettes."

"Like a coffee subscription box," she muttered, still staring at her empty mug. "New cigs every month."

James tried to imagine it but failed. Most smokers would want something more frequent, and many were loyal to their type. They didn't want to try new things.

Stephanie traced her finger on the rim of her coffee cup. Around and around and around. James caught his slow blink and stood up.

Why'd they have to be locked in a room with just a stupid Keurig? He could use an espresso right now. Christ, 12:30 in the morning, and no good ideas yet. He wanted to join the doctor on the floor and sleep, but James had a sneaking suspicion if he and Stephanie couldn't come up with something good, Harbor Stix would rescind its protection. He felt weird about being the reason why a cure for cancer didn't get made.

James plodded to the coffee machine and stuck his paper cup under the dispenser. How many had he drunk tonight? Four. God, it was a good thing coffee wasn't-

He spun, staring at Stephanie. She jerked her head up.

"What?"

"We can be like coffee."

"Subscriptions?"

"Addictive, but nobody cares! There's a ton of research about how caffeine is bad for you. And caffeine headaches! People get addicted cuz the consequences are worth it."

Stephanie pushed herself up, caught in the idea. "Lung cancer is a big thing that pushes people away."

"But if lung cancer is curable-"

"No more surgeon warnings. Could we market to kids again? We can be...the opposite of coffee. A smoke for stress relief. Addictive meditation."

"A PR campaign, using smokers as test subjects for the treatment -"

"Limiting the impact of smoking on health and erasing our biggest roadblock-"

"We'd need lobbyists and -"

"All the tobacco companies would be on board. It can be like Got Milk? Only Got a Stick?"

"The return of the smoke break."

A loud snore from the doctor broke through their conversation. Stephanie giggled, high on their idea.

"Let me get another cup of coffee, but I think we can put together a deck in the next two hours. Gives us...five hours of sleep before people show up."

"Perfect," James said. Saving smokers, making money. All part of the job.

Selkie Business

"**I**'m not giving you children." She crosses her arms. "You stole my coat. We're married. But I draw the line at producing babies with blubber cheeks to pinch."

You blush and stammer. "I wanted a partner to produce profits, not offspring."

She tilts her head. She doesn't have much of a neck, so it's more of a roll than a tilt.

"Your business is off to a very rocky start if you don't know the basis of a selkie contract."

You look down at the seal skin in your hands. To be fair, all the guy on the beach this morning had said was 'Selkies make the best partners. All you gotta do is find a skin.'

You look at your new wife through your fringe, hoping to hide your embarrassment. Your second wife. Ah. Shit.

She glares at you, naked as she stands on the sand. Dark skin, short rough hair. Rolls and short limbs. Bold enough that you feel naked.

The selkie sighs. "You're not aware of us, are you?"

"Selkies?"

"Any of the magic folk that live along here. You're a tourist."

You nod. "Came to look at a fishing boat."

She stares at the fur coat in your hand. You offer it to her, but she steps away.

"Magic has rules. You pick up a seal maiden's coat, you are wed. Most don't want a selkie wife, and so leave a coat alone when they find it. But you, damm. We're tied for life now."

"Divorce isn't an option?"

"Magical contracts are binding and unbreakable. I'm your wife."

"Like... legally?"

She blinks her large, brown eyes. "To me. To my people, yes. But not to yours."

"Okay, good. Because human law says I can't have two wives-"

"Well, you'll have to introduce us. I can't just swim off and never see you again. You have my coat. You'll be compelled to keep it near, and I'm tethered to it. You're not getting rid of me."

"Aaaand, can I introduce you as my business part-ner?" Maybe this can still work out.

"You agree to a childless marriage?"

"Between us? Yes."

"Fine. Partners in life and boats. At the very least, it's obvious you would sign any contract placed in front of you and you really shouldn't do that. All paperwork comes to me for approval."

You fidget. You've already bought a boat because you liked the name, only to realize it's not quite seaworthy just like you're not quite business-worthy. The man who sold you the boat and told you about Selkie Point probably deduced both facts in seconds.

You pull the rolled-up contract from your back pocket and hand it to your new partner. She looks at it and sighs.

"Okay, husband. Let's get started. I can tell you cannot do this alone."

Till Death

Jasper clutched his arm to his side. It felt broken in two places, quite a feat as his power came from his bones. Strength that didn't make him strong, but made him capable of enduring in ways other heroes could not.

The Gem Shield, his action figure claimed. The tank, his allies said.

The man at his end, Jasper thought. Twenty years of heroing. 16 to 36. Twenty years of fighting, of saving. Of absorbing blows and pushing teammates out of the way. Twenty years of injuries and twenty years of aging and trauma to his bones. Microfractures might help martial artists develop tough fists, but misdirecting car doors with your forearm took a toll.

Two breaks. In the same arm. That wouldn't have happened five years ago.

Jasper looked up. Angel Hair continued the fight, Obsidian supporting her as Enclave's minions protected the villain while she set up her machine. It'd be death for the city, trapping it behind a wall of technology and magic no power could break through. Trade halted, communication dead, no way to see in.

Jasper knew where the small test cities were. Had been. Completely closed off, the status of those inside unknown, they'd each been written off as lost. He refused to let his home be next.

But two breaks in his dominant arm. He can't punch with it, can't block. He'll be exposed, and it took less force to break a rib. Going back out there risked a punctured lung, risked death. He had always risked his life before, but it'd felt so unlikely. It doesn't now.

Jasper leaned against the alley wall and looked up at his fighting teammates. In their twenties and holding just fine.

He looked toward Enclave, unhurriedly pressing buttons. Could his teammates get to her without him? Possible, but then there would be questions. What happened? Why didn't he step back in? Being tired and scared weren't acceptable answers for a veteran hero, but for the first time, Jasper felt both in the middle of a fight. He wasn't invincible. His powers were weakening. He couldn't properly protect himself, let alone his teammates.

"Jasper?"

He whirled. One of the alley doors was open, the name of a tailor shop painted on it. A man in his early sixties peeked out, and seeing he had Jasper's attention, stepped into the alley.

"Stay inside, it's safer," Jasper said, but the man ignored him to come closer, eyes locked on Jasper's broken arm. Jasper dropped his grip on it and stood straight.

"You are hurt." The tailor had a Germanic hint to his voice, and in Jasper's mind he heard another, thicker German accent. A hero who had helped Jasper discover, use, and train his powers.

Hex had been his first and only mentor. Grief pulsed through Jasper at the reminder.

"I'm fine," Jasper said. "Just catching my breath and then I'll be back to stopping Enclave. Don't worry."

"Too late for that." The man pulled from his pocket a broken plastic hanger and a yellow flexible measuring tape. He reached for Jasper's arm and Jasper, wanting any kindness from the mirror of a loved one, held out his broken arm.

The man pushed the bones into place, Jasper did no more than grunt, and constructed a brace from a hanger and measuring tape.

"Stay put," he commanded the knot, and Jasper smiled. His daughter liked to command the world around her, using her limited vocabulary to convince crayons to stay on the table or the dog to sit. It's an ineffective ask here, the knot would last maybe ten minutes of movement. But it was a kindness, a hope for the brace to hold and do its job for as long as needed.

"Thank you," Jasper said.

"Thank you for fighting. But know, son, you do not have to fight forever. You can rest."

"I will rest very well tonight," Jasper assured him.

The man frowned. "Not what I meant." He dug into his pocket and pulled out a black business card. He slid it under the hem of Jasper's sleeve, and Jasper was impressed by the man's ability to pick out the seam between suit and glove.

"Be safe, Jasper," the man said.

Jasper nodded. He always tried to be. But now, caught by a civilian and with Angel Hair's cry of pain coming from the fight, Jasper had no excuse to linger on the ground. He jumped up on the fire escape to return to the rooftops, to the fight.

He came up on Enclave's least protected side and charged, good shoulder leading the way. Minions fell, bowled over like pins, and Jasper knocked Enclave away from the device's panel.

The resulting fight was awkward, having to both use his left hand and shield his right, but Jasper trained for situations like this and kickboxing was part of his regimen. Enclave went down, Angel Hair's prehensile lochs tying her up while Obsidian's power over darkness blinded the cursing villain.

The miracle of the fight was that the tailor's brace stayed put. The hanger pieces didn't shift. The measurement tape stayed tied. It was dumb luck, a miracle, or...

Hex had been named as such for his magical powers. They'd been particular, he'd only been able to control objects under five pounds, and it meant he won battles by cunning rather than prowess. Sticking shoes to the ground, directing fishing lines or pebbles.

Making sure braces stayed in place.

Jasper's breath hitched. He frantically went for the card the tailor slipped under his suit. It wasn't, as Jasper hoped, for the tailor's shop. It was Dr. Death's calling card.

Jasper didn't understand. Dr. Death was known as a hero killer and one of the few villains who operated on a national level. New York, Chicago, Tampa, rural Wyoming. Dr. Death had been the one to kill Hex.

Jasper flipped the card over. *For when you're tired,* it said.

And maybe, Jasper thought, the tailor didn't just remind him of Hex. Maybe he *was* Hex.

And maybe, that meant Jasper didn't have to be Jasper until his bones couldn't withstand the shocks anymore.

To Hold You Again

My sister died when she was eight. Bad heart, risky surgery. We gave thanks for what we got.

Medical bills racked up, Mom took on two jobs, Dad three, and I took on the house. Cleaning. Cooking.

Babysitting.

Kara had cried a lot. Pain, maybe. Discomfort. It was worse when she was a baby; she couldn't tell me what would make it better. That she needed a cuddle on the couch with cartoons. A painkiller. A distraction. She slept in my arms, be it in my bed or on the couch, and I knew her smells, her hair, her sighs, her hiccups.

I barely saw my parents, but I saw Kara all the time.

No one knew her cry like me.

And that's what I hear now. Crys from a fallen baby angel in a bed of crushed wild violets.

You're supposed to ignore fallen angels, let them cry. When a devil wanders up from a lava tube or the sewer system, no one cares. The world might try to balance the distribution of souls between demons, humans, and angels via a reincarnation cycle, but there's no reason to not let a demon live on the surface if they make it. It's kinder than Hell.

Heaven though. It's paradise. Angels rarely slum it on Earth, knowing their souls will land there eventually. The thing is though, fallen baby angels can't make it back up. So you're supposed to let them cry and cry and cry until an adult comes to carry them. Why would anyone want to deny a soul Heaven for a few decades or longer?

But the angel baby crying in the flower bed has Kara's cry, Kara's nose, Kara's dimple. She has things I'm not familiar with, downy wings and a new collection of moles, but it's her. I know it.

I only had eight years with her. Eight years that ended a month ago and it is second nature to pull out a toy from my bag. To place the soft doll in Kara's hand. To coo and pick her up and whisper everything is fine.

To walk home with her, singing her favorite lullaby.

The angel isn't Kara. I know that. There are no memories, no history, in her brain. New life, old soul.

But I want another eight years, sixteen, fifty. Angels have grown up on Earth before, made nests in penthouses and flown between skyscrapers. There's no harm in it, and who knows if Heaven really is better. It might be paradise, but Kara's angel parents obviously pay less attention to her than I did if she's fallen through the clouds.

Taking Kara home feels like payback, like peace, like a second chance.

I tuck her into her old bed and fall asleep beside her.

Baking Rites

I shaha is a baker because she's a morning person. She has no problem arriving slightly before dawn to start her work. Ishaha is also a crafter because she has good lungs and a strong throat and can talk for hours. Baking is a craft that takes a lot of time, after all.

Today she rushes through the gathering of her ingredients. Sleep had been hard to come by the previous night, an ache settling into her bones, and today that ache is worse. She scrunches her hands and holds back a cough. She wants to rush through work, as much as she can without risking the magic, and go home.

She measures her spell ingredients – flour, eggs, water, and a pinch of sugar. She mixes them– hands, spoon, and a punch for good luck before she sets aside fist-sized balls of dough to grow. Then, she starts feeding the oven.

This is where the magic comes into play. Her ingredients are mixed and prepped, now it's time to build up the needed energy. Ishaha lays the groundwork for the spell literally and audibly. Humming softly, warming up her voice, she lays the sticks in the appropriate chamber under the oven.

One on the left, one on the right. One on the left, one on the right. Small stacks, and then she arranges peat in a circle between them. She lights it on fire. The peat catches, and she moves on to the next part of the ritual. Humming a staccato beat to mirror the upcoming consumption of wood, Ishaha places larger pieces of wood in the chamber. First, one on either outer edge of her small piles, set down exactly seven beats apart. Once the small stacks alight, she slides in three more thick pieces of wood arranged in a fan, joint end away from her. Then, she shuts the door and starts the rite properly.

"Oh baking gods, warm this oven!" She bows before the clay shape. "Oh baking gods, warm this oven!" She bows again, a total of five chants matching the split logs newly placed.

Then she turns to the awaiting loaves. "Oh baking gods, merge with my creation." She bows before the bread, again completing five chants and bows.

She repeats the cycle five times, for a total of 50 chants and 50 bows.

The next step is add in two more pieces of wood. She does, then repeats her chats and bows, now in pairs. The gods must approve today because her bread dough is getting fat with their attention, full of divine energy. Ishaha's good at bakecraft - the gods always answer her.

She's getting tired though, the ache in her bones and the scratch in her throat turning troublesome, and the most physically demanding part of bake craft is just beginning. Ishaha smothers a cough in her elbow as she pulls out the oven rack. Then, she lifts the cloth off her loaves. Ishaha claps, picks up a loaf, and raises it to the sky. "Thank you for embodying this bake!" No bow this time, instead she twirls to showcase the risen loaf to the gods before placing it on the far-left corner of the rack.

Her eighth time saying the rite, she finishes with a cough. It should be alright, she'd said the words clearly. Ishaha rushes through the rest, forcing words and not coughs out of her mouth. She stumbles over the twelfth one, repeating the word 'thank' three times. She dearly hopes that doesn't ruin her crafting.

With a gloved hand, Ishaha opens the door and gently deposits her full rack of loaves on the clay shelf above the fire. A glance at the flames shows the gods are hungry, so she feeds it more wood before closing the door and begins the bulk of the rite.

Ishaha bends over, touches her toes, and then slowly trails her hands up her body until her fingers reach for the sky. "Grow!" she chants. "Expand!"

She opens her arms wide, gathering energy, and tosses it at the oven. "Divine heat, gift of the gods, fill this space!"

She bows, walks to the other side of the oven, and repeats. She has to do the chant thirty times on each side, and she manages the first few with no problem. But as Ishaha bends over for a toe touch, coughs rack her body. She jerks up, thumping her chest, trying to get air, and it's only after her body settles does she realizes she's not just interrupted the ritual, but stopped it. She doesn't remember her count. She's stopped chanting. She's lost the god's attention.

All that time, preparing the oven and bread, lost. Her perfect record of bakecraft, always having pleased the gods and gotten warm bread as a result, gone.

Another cough shutters in her chest and she forces it down. There have been too many disruptions! Maybe she can salvage this, but keeping her mouth closed hurts her chest. Ishaha's cough bursts out of her.

She cries. Oh, the bread is ruined now. So ruined. She collapses on a seat, sniffing as she watches the sunrise. Some baker she is. Some crafter, favored speaker to the gods.

She blames her distress for missing the smell at first. It wafts through her small workspace, warm and yeasty. Ishaha turns toward the oven; its heat has never gone away. Cautiously she grabs her glove and opens the door.

Her loaves are fat and oval, golden and baked. She pulls them out and cuts into one. It's airy and soft with a crisp crust. Ishaha pulls a slice to her face and *inhales*.

She doesn't understand. The rites were broken. Her calls to the gods interrupted. She stares at the open oven, at the ashes of her fire, the heat wavering before the door.

Did she only need to call the gods to heat the oven and fill the bread? But no, she'd coughed during the bread display. Minor, but a mar on how she'd wanted to cast her charm.

She holds her bread in hand. It's a beautiful loaf, and a nibble proves it's taste. All her bread loaves this bake look similar. Will probably taste this delicious. This is her best bake craft yet.

But it's not bake*craft*, she realizes. It's just...bake.

Ishaha eats her fresh bread. Her messed-up ritual had still produced perfect loaves.

Do the gods even listen to crafters?

She stares at the crumbs on her lap as the oven's warmth dissipates into the morning air.

Mothman, Bigfoot, & I

You yank on the extension cord, gripping the orange plastic as you march toward the end of the backyard.

"Do you want help?" Raora asks, keeping pace by taking tiny steps. You shake your head.

"It's like, those rope exercises, at the gym," you huff.

Raora looks back at the trailing extension cord, two fingers around and unraveling from the spool in the garage. Thankfully, she doesn't say anything. You know it's not exactly like the exercises you've seen in videos. Those ropes are as big as your forearms. But you have to start somewhere.

The cord yanks back. You've hit the end of the spool. Now, you turn to Raora for help. Her bigfoot eyes can see better in the dark than your human ones.

"Can you see the end of the light string?"

She finds it quickly and brings it over. There's not enough slack for the cords to lay on the ground, but that's okay. In mid-air, you connect them.

Power runs from the house, through the extension cord, through another seven extension cords, and then the dead tree you wrapped in a neighborhood's worth of Christmas lights blazes on.

You can sorta see it through the trees, the summer foliage makes it hard. You can however hear the squawk of birds, squirrels, and other creatures as the sudden appearance of the sun wakes them. More importantly, you hear a whisper on the wind, soft as feathers, and you know for you to have heard it this far away it had to have been shouted very, very loudly.

"LIGHT!"

Quickly, you unplug the cords. Raora snickers. "Oh, Mothman saw that alright."

You plug the lights back in, wait three seconds, and reintroduce the lights to power.

"LIGHT!"

You continue the pattern, plugging and unplugging the lights. You can't hear Mothman very well, but you can imagine them staring at the tree with wide, round eyes then turning around frantically when you turn the tree off. Raora's hearing is better, and she shakes her head.

"He's in awe every. Single. Time. It's kinda adorable."

"He needs a girlfriend," you say.

"He gets distracted by every car that goes by after dark."

"Isn't that why you told him to not leave the woods? And he's listened, he hasn't left the woods in a year."

Underneath her fur, you think she's blushing.

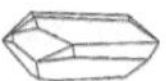

You get in trouble - stealing the neighborhood's Christmas lights, wasting power, climbing dead trees. You're grounded for the rest of the summer, and none of the cryptids in the woods take the risk to visit. Raora tried, once, but got mistaken for a bear and someone called animal control.

Mom makes you go through safety classes, puts you on the couch and forces you to watch video after video of the dangers of being in the woods. Bear attacks and wolf attacks and poisonous mushrooms. You brush it off, but something must have stuck because when summer rolls around again, when you have free time all day, when you peek into the woods and see something staring back, you turn on your heels and rush back into the house.

There's the sound of a pebble hitting your window. You look up, giddy. Hoping that after confessing to Geoff at the homecoming game earlier before running off, he'd come over to say he liked you too.

There's another pebble. You push aside your curtain to look out the window and -

The full power of a Dodge Ram LED high beam streams into your eyes and you fall back, too shocked to even scream, but then the light is gone. You blink at the stars in your eyes, wondering if what you saw was real. How would a light get that high? Why?

It's not real.

You move to the window, only to be blasted with light again and this time you cry in pain. The light immediately shuts off.

"I don't think humans like light like you do, dear."

"Light," someone says mournfully.

"Let's try this one," the first voice says.

There's a softer light outside the window, and when you look something is hovering in the air covered in fairy lights. Not something, *someone.*

"Mothman," you breathe. Suddenly, you can't forgive yourself for never visiting in years. For forgetting that all the friends you had in the woods were real.

You open the window and there's Raora on the grass, holding the light string as if Mothman was a light-up balloon.

She waves. "Ignoring us wasn't a good prank," she says.

You sob because it wasn't a prank. And you think she knows that, even if Mothman doesn't.

"Sorry," you say. "But I like this one."

You smile at her, and then at Mothman. His fuzzy antennae wiggle. "More light?" his hands hold a spotlight.

"No, no. I've had enough light," you say. "But not enough of you. I'll be right there."

Rider's Three

I don't expect the piercing pain of the sun. I roll over, turning away from it, and fall off an edge. I flail, skirts snapping in the air, then find myself upright and sitting on the rump of a white stallion pressed against a saddle. The stallion takes no notice of my sudden weight. The man in the saddle, dressed in white matching his horse, also says nothing about the fact I am now behind him, my thin arms around his waist.

He glows faintly. Or perhaps the horse does. I glance at my bare forearm against the rider's side, skin its standard summer tan but lacking the glow of my new companion.

I look up. Left. Right. All around us are dark, tall forms. It's hard to tell with the limited light and my recent sun blindness, but I think they are trees stripped bare of leaves. Those beside us are an ash gray, while the trees before us are a dark midnight that blends into shadows. I start to turn to see the trees behind us, curious as to their color, but the white rider places a hand on mine and squeezes.

"What are you doing?" he asks.

"Learning," I reply.

"Why do you want to learn?"

"Is it not enough to simply want to?"

He chuckles. His voice is morning-rough, his hands chilled.

"Is that what you want? To learn?"

I remember reading by candlelight. Experimenting with herbs in food and tinctures, tastes and effects. "More than anything."

"Very well," the white rider says. "But don't look behind us. You cannot learn all at once, lest you get overwhelmed. Learn slow, learn right. Make your guesses and then prove them. Safely."

I tighten my arms around his waist and lean over, my unbound hair scratching my cheek. The stallion may be white, but his hooves are golden. They illuminate where he treads, over the gnarled roots of an old-growth forest. The horse steps and a glow grows from his print. The soil shifts from midnight to mulberry to ember before settling into a rich brown. When he steps next, I pay attention to a tree beside us. Its color changes are more subtle, shadows deepening, bark edges highlighted in gold.

The stallion's hoofprints are mini sunsets, bringing light to the world. I turn, eager to watch the morning colors bloom behind me.

Pain blooms in my head. I slam my eyelids down. I knew what followed us, yet I turned to stare into the sun anyway. The rider laughs.

"You don't need your eyes to learn. There are other senses."

The rider's voice has changed, but he is the same girth under my hands. The sun-warmth on my back has disappeared.

"What have you learned?" he asks in a smooth voice.

"That the white rider and his steed bring the sun."

"What else?" the second rider prods.

"That learning can be painful."

He laughs a second time. It doesn't feel like he is making fun of me, but I can't be sure. It's a stranger's laugh. It smarts anyway. I expect him to ask again about the information I'm gathering; if I know who the white rider is, if I know who he is. Because I do. I do, I do.

The rider asks a more important question. "Will pain stop you from learning?"

I remember stomach cramps and the scratches of thorns. Embers on my palms, catching skin between my mortar and pestle. Freshly washed berries and later dizziness. Each injury a bit of knowledge.

"No."

Keeping my eyes closed, I take in our surroundings. The horse is walking down a shallow slope, the rider barely leaning into me. The cloth of his jacket is still fine, still smooth, just like the other rider's. His posture, however, isn't as upright, I can detect the slight bow in his back. The stallion, too, has a less springy gait. This is no fresh rider. He and his mount have been riding all day.

"Look back, and open your eyes."

I crane my neck around and do as he commands. Behind us stretches a well-lit forest. No, not quite. The green nearest me is vibrant but fades four trees back. The stallion is red, his rider clad in the same color. I look down at the horse's hooves. They glow, but unlike the white stallion the red stallion's glow orange and the effect isn't steady. I watch the horse lift a glowing hoof, the light dying, only to reappear when the hoof touches the earth. The soil transitions from chocolate to charcoal with each light-leaching step.

I lean my forehead on the rider's back, forgoing any attempt to look around him at the path ahead. I know better, feel the warmth on the bare back of my hands. The white rider brings the sun, the red rider pushes it away.

"You learn quickly," the red rider says.

"I remember well," I answer.

"And when you don't?" a third voice, the third rider asks.

The world shifts, even as I don't. I'm still on a horse. My arms are still around a rider, but my vision has gone. I squeeze the man before me. He's wearing a coat trimmed in fur and when a breeze blows across the back of my neck, I wish for the same. I expect he is dressed in black to match his mount.

"How will you learn," the black rider asks me. His voice is deep and tired. "If there's no path to see? If you are stumbling in the dark with no direction?"

I'm not blind, I realize. There is simply no light.

There's a soft rustling, wind through the trees. I hear hooves on earth, on wood, on stone. A low murmuring, a nearby stream whose constant noise means we are following it. I'm still in the forest. The rider's chest under my hands is thin and frail. His horse moves slowly, almost shuffling. Something brushes my cheek and I jerk. The other riders followed an invisible path, twisting around trunks and avoiding branches. That path is gone now, just like the light, and the woods crowd close. I scrunch up to avoid the reaching branches.

Stars stretch across the sky, bright and numerous. As my eyes adjust, I can see the shape of trees on either side of us, but only a few. There are no golden hooves, no light but the pinpricks above.

I remember having no teacher, no one to take me in, though I asked. Watching others in the village from afar, observing animals, making guesses. Learning to live.

"Learning doesn't need a path," I say, staring at the stallion bob his head. He's black like the space between stars, the shadow of caves. I can't see into the air inches before his muzzle. "You are your own guide and travel where you will. Step by step."

"You will learn well, witchling," the black rider says. "Is there something you wish to learn from me?"

I grin because with the third rider's question I know I have passed. I've been approved by all three riders and thus their master.

What I want, what I've always wanted, is to under-stand the world. To have knowledge in my head and the ability to practice it. And while I don't need a teacher, I want one because there are limits to what I can teach myself.

I ask for the ultimate source of knowledge. "Where's the location of the chicken-legged house?"

"Why, it is here."

The stallion stops. I'm no longer sitting behind a saddle with my arms around a rider. I'm standing before a small wooden hut. It is narrow and the legs it stands on tall. I turn back to the black rider.

I can't see his face in the dark. He and the stallion blend into the night, the glint of starlight on the bridle and their steaming breath my only clue where to look.

"Take your step, witchling."

He urges the horse forward. I turn and move my left foot forward.

I travel again. Morning. Evening. Night. White. Red. Black. Three steps, three lessons, three riders. When I get to the front of the house, the chicken legs bend down and the door opens.

It's lit from within by dozens of floating candle flames. There's a stew on the fire I can smell, mush-rooms and pine. Familiar herbs hang on the back of the door. The woman barely lit in the doorway is slim, her skirt short enough to show off legs thin as bones.

"I've come to learn from you, Baba Yaga," I say.

"And what would I teach you that you cannot learn yourself?"

"All that I do not know."

"And what of that which I do not know?"

"If you don't know it, it's not worth knowing."

She laughs. "What do you want to be?"

"Learned. Respected." I think of the word the villagers have called me, what the riders have labeled me as, and own it as my third answer. "A witch."

"If you can find me again through the liminal forest, I will teach you. Step one, witchling. Wake up."

My eyes water from the light. I'm on my back, facing the bright blue sky. There's a breeze on my cheek, fuzz on my teeth, a weakness in my bones, but my mind is mighty and clear. I push myself up on my elbows carefully. I'm on a platform, wrapped in soft cloth, feet above the ground. The four posts are sturdy, supported by short angled pieces of wood.

A sky burial platform.

I look around at the other platforms, the other bodies, but I'm the only person moving. We've been left here to dry out, to turn to bone. I'm not ready for the end. I have so much to learn. So much I want to know.

I dangle my feet off the edge of the platform and fall, rolling to absorb the impact. Above me, my platform looks like the elevated floor of a narrow house, the bracing legs remind me of chicken claws. I'll be back, one day, when I can build the walls and make it move.

For now, I turn to the woods. I have a long walk ahead of me and no rider's horse to share. I remember the roots and stones beneath the white horse gaining color. I remember the slope the red horse walked down. I remember the stream the black horse plodded alongside.

Find me again, Baba Yaga had said.

The sun is rising. I set out walking, determined to prove I learned my first lessons.

Previous Publications

Most of these stories have been published previously.

Some I initially released to subscribers as part of a series called Roll to Plot, where I used dice rolls to select the genre, antagonist, and a notable item based on lists provided by followers. Others are prompt fills from accounts on Tumblr, usually @writing-prompt-s or @deepwaterwritingprompts.

Others were originally published in anthologies where my story was simply one of many. These are:

- Undine's Paladin, originally published in *Denizens in the Deep*. 2022

- Riders Three, originally published in *Triple Vision*. 2021.

Thank You For Reading

One of the joys of being an author is seeing readers reactions to my work. I hope you enjoyed this short story collection, and I ask for just a simple favor if you did – to rate it on Amazon, Goodreads, or Storygraph.

Ratings help indie authors like myself a lot – readers use them to determine future reads and they can provide an algorithm boost on e-retailers. If you want to help future readers further, please leave a review! Let people know your favorite story and your experience reading this collection to let a future reader know what to expect.

About Gwen

Gwen Tolios is an asexual author from Chicago, who enjoys writing queer stories. She lives with her cat, Shady, who refuses to cuddle but certainly likes to scream.

While primarily known for her short fiction, Gwen has also written the sapphic romance *Returning to You* and has released creative nonfiction under the penname Virginia Mueller.

Keep in Touch

You can find Gwen on social media around the web as @GwenTolios, or @Gwen-Tolios on Tumblr. She releases short stories for free on her Tumblr, and currently has an ongoing series on her Substack titled Chicago's Grimm – reimagining Grimm's fairy tales as modern fantasy stories set in Chicago.

Sign up for her newsletter – Gwen's Writing Gossip – to get updates, free stories, and a free book!

Scan the QR code below for her Linktree: https://linktr.ee/gwentolios